Rules for Secret keeping

ALSO BY LAUREN BARNHOLDT

The Secret Identity of Devon Delaney
Devon Delaney Should Totally Know Better
Four Truths and a Lie

Rules for Secret Keeping

LAUREN BARNHOLDT

BARRINGTON AREA LIBRARY
505 N. NORTHWEST HWY.
BARRINGTON, ILLINOIS 60010

Aladdin
New York   London   Toronto   Sydney

ALADDIN

An imprint of Simon & Schuster Children's Publishing Division

1230 Avenue of the Americas, New York, NY 10020

First Aladdin hardcover edition October 2010

Copyright © 2010 by Lauren Barnholdt

All rights reserved, including the right of reproduction in whole or in part in any form.

ALADDIN is a trademark of Simon & Schuster, Inc., and related logo is a registered trademark of Simon & Schuster, Inc.

For information about special discounts for bulk purchases, please contact Simon & Schuster Special Sales at 1-866-506-1949 or business@simonandschuster.com.

The Simon & Schuster Speakers Bureau can bring authors to your live event. For more information or to book an event contact the Simon & Schuster Speakers Bureau at 1-866-248-3049 or visit our website at www.simonspeakers.com.

Designed by Jessica Handelman

The text of this book was set in Lomba Book.

Manufactured in the United States of America 0810 FFG

10 9 8 7 6 5 4 3 2 1

Full CIP data for this book is available from the Library of Congress.

ISBN 978-1-4169-8020-9

ISBN 978-1-4424-0954-5 (eBook)

For my dad

ACKNOWLEDGMENTS

Thanks to my editor, Kate Angelella, for always knowing what's best for the book and being so absolutely amazing to work with.

Alyssa Henkin, for being the best agent a girl could ask for—"thank you" doesn't even begin to cover it!

My husband, Aaron, for everything—I love you.

My mom, for constantly sending me emails about what to blog about—thanks for always being there for me.

My sisters, Krissi and Kelsey, for being my best friends.

Jodi Yanarella, Scott Neumyer, Kevin Cregg, and the Govine family for their support.

Jessica Burkhart—TEAM BARNHART FTW!

Mandy Hubbard for Text in the City, and answering all my crazy emails.

And, of course, all the girls who read the Devon books or *Four Truths and a Lie* and emailed me to tell me how much you liked them—it means more than you know. ☺

One

ON THE FIRST DAY OF SEVENTH GRADE,
I open my locker before homeroom to find a note from
Eric Niles, which says the following:

> *Dear Samantha,*
> *You look really pretty today.*
> *Love,*
> *Your Secret Admirer*

In kindergarten, Eric and I got seated next to each
other by accident when the teacher thought I was a boy,
since they'd mistakenly printed "Sam" on the class list
instead of my full name, "Samantha." Eric didn't want to
sit next to a girl, so he burst into tears, and then *I* burst
into tears, and Eric felt so bad that at recess he picked

me a dandelion flower and asked me to marry him. Ever since then, he's been kind of like my stalker. But not the really crazy kind you have to get a restraining order against or anything. More like the slightly obsessive, slightly annoying kind you roll your eyes at and try to tolerate.

"Is that from Eric?" my best friend, Daphne, says, coming up behind me. She peers over my shoulder at the paper. "How does he know you look really pretty today? Has he even *seen* you yet?" She takes a good look at my first-day-of-school outfit—jean skirt, leggings, black-and-white-striped top, and huge earrings. "Although you do look pretty cute."

"Daphne, this is Eric we're talking about." I place the note back in my locker and slam it shut. "Since when has sanity ever been his thing?"

"True."

"And why does he always sign them 'Your Secret Admirer'?" I ask. "I know it's him. I recognize his handwriting."

"I think you're too hard on him," Daphne says. "He's not *that* bad. Last year in math, I was constantly asking him if I could borrow some paper, and he never even once got mad."

"Daphne, he eats paste."

"He hasn't done that since third grade," Daphne says. And then her green eyes crinkle up at the edges and she gives me a look. One of those looks people give you when they've figured something out that you don't necessarily want them to know, and now they're going to tease you about it. "Oohh," she says. "I know what this is about. This is about Jake."

I try to look haughty. "No, it isn't!" I bend down and pretend to be tying my shoe so she doesn't see the look that's running across my face, which basically means that, yes, it is about Jake. "Have you seen him yet?" I straighten up and shrug my shoulders. "Just, you know, out of curiosity."

"Nope," Daphne says. "Guess he's not here yet."

Jake's our best friend. Well, he *was* our best friend, until the end of last year when suddenly I decided that he and I should be more than best friends. (This was spurred on by what I like to call The Scandalous Skateboard Incident, or TSSI for short. Daphne doesn't like referring to it as TSSI since she thinks it sounds kind of like a disease. Ever since Daphne's orthodontist told her she might have TMJ, which is some kind of teeth-grinding affliction, she doesn't like referring to things by their initials. Medical conditions make her nervous.)

The Scandalous Skateboard Incident (or TSSI for

those who aren't freaked out by anagrams that may or may not remind them of diseases) happened at the beginning of the summer, right before Jake left for camp. One night, he invited me and Daphne over to his house to skateboard. This wasn't the scandalous part—Jake was always inviting Daphne and me over to skateboard, although none of us actually skateboarded except him. Usually we'd sit on his porch and read magazines while Jake constructed some sort of ramp or obstacle course in his garage. Then Jake would emerge and try to do stunts on whatever sort of contraption he'd built.

Anyway, on the day of TSSI, Jake was in his garage building a ramp out of some drywall and a traffic cone that he *said* he'd ordered off the internet, but that I think he stole when he got his driveway paved in the spring, and Daphne and I said we were leaving, because we were bored of reading magazines. And then Jake said, no, no, the ramp was done, and we should all go out into the road and watch him try it out. Daphne and I agreed, since we actually do like to watch Jake skateboard (he always does lots of tricks and flips and then we get to give him a score on a scale of one to ten, kind of like Olympic judges), we just don't like waiting around while he builds things.

So we all traipsed out to the road, and Jake set up the

ramp, and after a few times of having to move it since cars were coming, we had it all set and ready to go. And Jake started off down the street so he could build up speed, and he came racing toward the ramp, and then he went up, up, up, and jumped a little bit in the air to grab the bottom of his board, and then floated down to the ground and skated to a stop right in front of us. It was amazing, exactly like something you'd see on one of those crazy extreme sports shows on TV.

So then I said that I wanted to try it, and Jake and Daphne both gave me a look, because I am very unco-ordinated and also because I had never once shown any interest in skateboarding. But Jake also looked impressed, and so I got on the board, but when I went over the ramp, I got thrown off somehow and ended up on the pavement with a scraped elbow and a slightly bloody lip.

Jake and Daphne rushed over, and when I looked up, I don't know what it was, but Jake was bent over me and the sun was shining, making a halo of light behind his head, and he looked so cute and concerned, and some-thing started in my heart and I knew then that noth-ing would ever be the same. Okay, so that's dramatic, but I knew that I liked him, at least. But then I had to go home because I was bleeding, and Jake left the next morning for camp and I haven't seen him since. Daphne says maybe the only reason I think I like him is because I had a brain injury when I fell off that skateboard.

"In fact," Daphne's saying now, "I haven't really seen *anyone* from our school yet."

Our locker and homeroom numbers were sent to us over the summer, in an effort to "limit confusion on the first day of school," and so all around us, kids are running up and down the halls, looking for their lockers. All the elementary schools in the district feed into Millboro Middle School, but so far, except for Daphne, I haven't seen one familiar face. Daphne and I survey the chaos in front of us, searching for people we know.

"Oh, look!" I say. "There's Ronald Hughes!" We watch as Ronald Hughes, a kid from our elementary school, runs down the hall, screaming, "Welcome to middle school!" and making ape noises. Hmm. Not exactly the best representation of our elementary school, but whatever.

"Wow," Daphne says. "He really does sound like an ape." Ronald adds a stomp to his routine, and now people are actually moving out of his way and staring. I can't help but feel a little bit of pride. I do know him, after all.

"Oh!" Daphne says as Ronald disappears around the corner at the end of the hall. "I almost forgot. Look what I made you." She opens her binder and pulls out a piece of shiny pink paper. "It's an advertisement for your secret-passing business."

I look down at the flyer.

HAVE A SECRET YOU JUST *NEED* TO GET OUT? IS YOUR BEST FRIEND'S NEW BACK-TO-SCHOOL SHIRT A TOTAL FASHION DON'T? WANNA ANONYMOUSLY TELL YOUR CRUSH YOU LIKE HIM?

Save yourself the embarrassment and pass your secret through me, Samantha Carmichael. Drop your secret along with a dollar into locker number 321, and it will be delivered to the recipient of your choice. **YOUR SECRET WILL NOT BE READ.**

Please do not forget to specify a name, as it is impossible to deliver secrets without knowing who they are for.

To ensure confidentiality, you may want to consider disguising your handwriting or printing your secret from a computer.

"These are awesome!" I squeal, running my finger over the navy blue letters.

"I figured we could hang these up around school,

since a lot of the kids from the other schools won't have heard of you."

Last year, in sixth grade, I started my own secret-passing business. Basically, kids would leave a note in my locker along with a dollar, and I'd pass the note to whomever they wanted. I never read the secrets, and it was totally anonymous. By the end of the year I'd made enough money to buy myself an iPod and pretty much a whole new wardrobe.

The bell rings then, and Daphne carefully places the sheet back into her binder. "Do you wanna hang out tonight?" she asks, as the throng of kids around us starts moving in an effort to get to homeroom. "We could discuss the day."

"Can't," I say. "I'm going into the city for my photo shoot." Recently I found out that I'm going to be featured in an upcoming issue of *You Girl* magazine (motto: America's number one tween magazine) as one of the finalists for its Young Entrepreneur of the Year award. My dad entered me in the competition a few months ago, and last week we got the call that I made it through to the next round. It's supposedly this really big deal, with a big banquet in a few weeks to pick the winner. I'm excited, but it's also a little nerve-racking. Last year's winner sold cloth bracelets or something to help the situation in Darfur. All I do is pass scandals and gossip. So not the same thing.

"I'll call you later, then," Daphne says. Then she grabs my arm, looks me in the eyes, and says, "Good luck" very dramatically before turning on her heel and heading in the direction of her homeroom. I take a deep breath and turn toward my own homeroom, room 167. Here goes nothing.

tw♥

I PICK A SEAT IN THE MIDDLE OF THE
room, halfway back, next to a friendly-looking girl who's
doodling flowers in her notebook. I decide it's time to
make new friends, since I still haven't seen anyone from
my old elementary school.

"Hi," I say, sliding into my seat and giving her a
friendly smile. I read in *You Girl* that if you want to make
new friends, you have to step out of your comfort zone
and be proactive and smiley. "I'm Samantha."

"Hi," she says, smiling back. "I'm Charlie." Wow.
Charlie. For a girl. What a cool name. "It's short for
Charlea," she says, as if she's reading my mind. "But
everyone calls me Charlie."

Wow. Even cooler. I wonder if I should change my
name to Sam? Sammi? Samara? My mom doesn't like

shortened names. "I named you Samantha," she says. "And if I wanted people to call you 'Sam,' that's what I would have named you. Or I would have had a boy."

"I like your shoes, Samantha," Charlie says, glancing down at my pink Skechers.

"Thanks." I pull a light blue spiral notebook out of my bag and open it to the first page, getting set to write down any important information about middle school that might be given to us in homeroom. My schedule is taped to the inside of the notebook so I don't lose it. I'm not so good at hanging on to important things, so I figured I'd better tape it down. But then my older sister, Taylor, pointed out that I would probably just lose the notebook, which wasn't very nice of her, but then she let me borrow her Skechers, so I kind of halfway forgave her.

"Hi!" Charlie suddenly squeals next to me. I'm so surprised I almost jump out of my seat.

"Hi!" I say back, confused since we already said that. Then I realize she's not talking to me. She's talking to another girl who's just walked into the room. The girl has crazy curly red hair that reaches all the way down her back, a short nose, and large green eyes. She's wearing a pair of jeans and a soft gray and pink sweater that dips down over one shoulder. On her head is a pink beret. A PINK BERET. As in, those weird hats they wear in France. You'd think she'd look silly, but somehow, she's able to pull it off. It looks cool and trendy, as if she's about to walk into a café and order a cappuccino or something. Most of the boys in the room turn to stare, and most of the girls do too.

Pink Beret rushes over to Charlie. "Charlie!" she says. "I tried IMing you last night, but my mom was being a total nightmare, she just—" And then she catches sight of me, and she stops talking.

"Hi," I say, giving her my we-should-be-friends smile. "I'm Samantha." How cool is this? First day of school, homeroom even, and I already have two new friends! Two cool new friends, who wear berets and have moms that are total nightmares. Not that I'll forget my old friends of course, that would be very mean of me. I'll have to plan a joint sleepover or something.

"Oh." Pink Beret ignores my introduction and puts a hand on her hip. She doesn't seem to be carrying any school supplies. What if she needs to take notes and write down important information pertaining to middle school? Hmm. I wonder if I have an extra pen. "You're in my seat."

"What?" How can I be in her seat? Has the teacher already assigned seats? Did I miss some sort of before-school mailing that alerted everyone to where they would be sitting in homeroom for the year?

"Oh," I say. "I didn't know we had assigned seats." Next to me, Charlie shifts uncomfortably.

"We don't," Pink Beret says. "But that's my seat."

I'm confused. "Hi," I try again. "My name's Samantha."

"I heard you the first time. And you, Samantha. Are. In. My. Seat." What can I do? I get up and move over. I mean, wow. I didn't know middle school was going to have a seat dictator. The worst part is that since everyone watched Pink Beret walk into the room, they all saw the horrible exchange in which she kicked me out of my own seat! Honestly, kind of a lot of people were watching. But that's okay. I'm regrouping. I'm calm. No need to panic. In fact, I'll just—

And at that moment, Jake walks into the classroom, plops down next to me, smiles, and says, "Hey." I'm so shocked that for a second, I can't answer. Jake is not supposed to be in my homeroom. He's supposed to be in room 241. I know because Daphne and I ran into his mom over the summer at the grocery store and she told us (after a little bit of prodding and a slight stalker mission in which we followed her down the cookie aisle and ended up having to spend all our allowance on five bags of Oreos).

"I didn't know you were going to be in my home-room," I blurt.

"I didn't either," he says, "but there was some sort of mix-up with my schedule." He's wearing long board shorts and a long-sleeved blue T-shirt and his brown hair is all mopsy and cute and his eyes look the same as when he looked at me during The Scandalous Skateboard Incident.

"Oh, well," I say, trying to sound coy. "Their mix-up is our gain." I give him a look with my eyebrows, but he just looks a little confused. Maybe because my eyebrows aren't completely grown in from when I tried to pluck them myself over the summer. They're *almost* grown in—honestly, you really can't even tell—but maybe I shouldn't be using them to convey meaningful looks. "How was camp?" I had figured I might get all tongue-tied when I saw Jake, and the first thing I would say is, "Hey, did you know I like you now?" because it would be on my brain. But honestly I'm pretty much fine. Not freaking out even a little bit.

Well, except for when Jake smoothes his hair away from his face and says, "It was all right. But I missed you guys." I missed you guys! Obviously by "you guys" he means me and Daphne, of course, but he probably only means ME, since, hello, I'm the one who wrote him a few postcards over the summer (just a few, no need to seem needy), and Daphne only sent him one very short note for his birthday.

"Cool," I say. "We missed you, too." *We missed you, too!* How cool is that to say? Am I flirting? I read an article about flirting in Taylor's *Spark* magazine (America's number one teen magazine), and it seemed horribly complicated. But maybe I'm a natural.

"How was your summer?" he asks.

"Not bad," I say. "I found out I'm a finalist for the *You Girl* Young Entrepreneur of the Year award."

"That's awesome," he says.

"Yeah, I have to go to New York after school today to get my picture taken for the magazine."

He laughs. "You're going to be in *You Girl*?"

"Yeah. Well, not just me. All the other finalists too." I try to raise my voice a little so that Pink Beret might overhear and be all, *Wow, you're going to be a famous model in America's number one tween magazine?* but she just keeps talking to Charlie, oblivious.

"That should be interesting."

"Interesting?"

"Yeah. Since you hate getting your picture taken."

This is true. I do hate getting my picture taken. "Well, I don't *hate* it exactly, I just—"

"Remember in third grade when you had to get your school picture retaken, like, ten times?" He laughs. I *did* have to get my picture retaken a bunch of times, but it wasn't my fault. The photographer kept telling me to look at this one spot above the camera, and every time I did, the flash would blind me. Plus they kept giving out these little plastic combs before taking your picture, and they'd encourage you to comb your hair, and for some reason, my hair always ended up sticking up.

"Ten times?" Pink Beret pipes up from her seat next to us. Oh, *now* she's listening. Of course. "That's crazy." She leans over the back of her chair, and her sweater dips down, revealing more of her shoulder, which is very tan. How is her shoulder tan? I thought redheads only burned. I'll bet it's fake.

"It wasn't *ten*," I say, feeling my face go red.

"It wasn't," Jake agrees, flashing his perfect smile at Pink Beret. She leans over farther, and now her stupid fake tan shoulder is almost right in Jake's face.

"Thank you," I say, shooting her a triumphant look.

"It was more like five." Jake winks at me. Pink Beret and Charlie giggle.

And they keep giggling when our homeroom teacher, Mr. Levin, comes in and welcomes us to Somerville Middle School. They giggle all during the morning announcements, and all during the pledge of allegiance. And when the bell rings, and Jake squeezes my arm and says, "See you later, Samantha," they don't even notice because they're already gone.

By the end of the day, I'm beginning to think that maybe middle school isn't all it's cracked up to be. In gym class we have to change. Which is fine, except that all the girls are wearing bras. I don't need a bra. Usually I just wear a sports bra under my clothes, but apparently even the girls who don't need bras are wearing real bras and then changing into sports bras. No one alerted me to this system (it really should have been revealed to us in our back-to-school mailing—locker number, homeroom, and bra situation).

We also get homework on the first day of school in math and English, which is just ridiculous. Daphne is in my lunch but none of my other classes, and except for homeroom and a few times in the halls, I don't see Jake again, but Charlie and her dumb red-haired friend are in my science, math, and gym classes. Of course.

When I finally get home, I just want to curl up and take a nice nap before the *You Girl* shoot, but my mom, who has the uncanny ability to pick the worst possible moment to decide to do something she thinks will be fun, has announced she's taking me to get my eyebrows waxed before she and my stepdad, Tom, drop me off at the train station for the photo shoot.

So the three of us pile into the car and head over to Wave, this totally cool spa and salon near our house. (My mom wanted to go to her fave salon, Candy's Curl, but luckily Ruth, their eyebrow waxer, was out for the day.) Once we're in Wave, Tom settles into a chair and starts flipping through a magazine (*Vogue*, which is weird, since, you know, he's a guy), and my mom marches me right up to the reception stand, where she begins talking in tones way too loud for an activity that is so embarrassing.

"We need an eyebrow waxing," she declares. "For a thirteen-year-old." She grabs me by the shoulder and pushes me forward. The receptionist, whose name tag says "Jemima," looks at my eyebrows and nods. "Now, normally," my mom says, "I would think that this was unnecessary for someone her age, but as you can see, she tried to pluck them herself."

Jemima nods again. "We get a lot of self-pluckers in here." Is this supposed to make me feel better? That there are a lot of self-pluckers? That's kind of like saying, "A lot of people wear hideous clothes." Just because a lot of people are doing something doesn't mean you necessarily want to be grouped in with them.

"Now, we don't want anything too *nuts*," my mom instructs. "Just a fix-up. No craziness like pink eyebrows or anything." She leans in a little closer to Jemima. "She's going to a photo shoot in the city, and she needs to look fabulous!"

Jemima looks me up and down, and I can tell she's wondering what kind of photo shoot I could possibly be going to, but thankfully, she doesn't ask. And even more thankfully, she pulls me into the back and away from my mom.

"Now," she says, pulling out a huge mirror and shoving it in front of my face. It makes every single pore look like a crater. I try not to look, but she's, like, pretty much forcing me. "Unfortunately, you've done a very bad job with your eyebrows."

Geez. Tell me what you really think. "I know," I say. "But, see, they were getting kind of bushy, and—"

"Mmm-hmm," she says, nodding. Her ears are pierced all the way up her ear. How cool. I only have one hole that I got a long time ago, when I was little. I want to get a second one, but I'm afraid of the pain.

"Now, this is going to be a two-step process," Jemima says. She sits me down in a chair and leans me back. "First I'm going to wax you. Then I'm going to shade you."

"Okay," I say uncertainly. Waxing and shading doesn't sound fun. Not even close. In fact, it sounds kind of horrible. Jemima starts putting something hot and sticky on one of my brows. Well, maybe I should consider this a lesson. Like how people are always saying that you should learn from every experience. And I've learned that I should definitely not try plucking my own eyebrows. How will I ever learn to eye flirt with Jake if I can't even keep my eyebrows in the right shape? In fact, I should probably—

"Oww!" I scream. A burning sensation is radiating from my eyebrows all the way down my face. Jemima has just ripped my skin right off my forehead.

I'm so loud that Tom comes running over from where he's been reading *Vogue*. "Are you okay?" he asks. He looks at Jemima suspiciously, but she calmly takes another dab of hot wax and starts putting it on my other brow.

"She's fine," Jemima says. "She's just not used to the *sensation*."

"Yeah, if you call ripping skin off my face a sensation." Ow. That really hurt.

"You can stop if you want, Samantha," Tom says, narrowing his eyes at Jemima, like he thinks she's some kind of torturer.

"She can't really," Jemima says cheerfully. "Then she'll be uneven."

"There are worse things to be," Tom says, "than uneven."

"I'm fine," I tell him, and after one last look, he turns and walks back to his chair. Okay, no big deal. I'll just concentrate on breathing in and out, like I learned when I took yoga in gym last year. It was all about relaxing. We even had a—

"Owww!" I scream as Jemima does the second eyebrow. I watch as she throws a little piece of paper with eyebrow hairs attached to it into the garbage. "Aren't you supposed to at least warn me? So I can, you know, prepare myself?"

"Next time," she says. "Now, listen. Since you're a self-plucker, the waxing has left you a little sparse. So you're going to have to shade a little bit." She pulls an eyebrow pencil off a cart on her left and opens it. "Do you know what this is?"

"Of course," I say. "It's an eyebrow pencil."

"Good." She nods. "Now, look in the mirror, and watch what I'm doing." I watch as she moves her hands in little flicks over my eyebrows, shading them in until they're perfect. Wow. Jemima's an artist.

"Wow," I say.

"You can have this pencil, but it's only a trial size," she says, handing it to me. "You should buy one at the front desk."

I hop out of the chair and practice wiggling my eyebrows in front of the mirror. I will most definitely be able to convey meaningful looks with these brows. These eyebrows will be able to say *I miss you as more than a friend* and *Let's hold hands* and *You should ask me to the dance, Jake*. These are the eyebrows of someone who knows how to flirt like an expert.

I'm spending so much time admiring my new brows that when Jemima clears her throat behind me, I jump. "Oh," I say. "Um, I was just making sure they were even." I clear my throat, like I was totally checking up on her work instead of admiring myself.

"Mmm-hmm," she says, sighing. "I'll meet you up front so I can show you what kind of pencil to buy before you pay."

I walk to the front of the salon, resisting the impulse to check myself out in the mirrors that are lining the walls. When I get to the waiting area, my mom is talking to a tall woman with long blond hair. Probably someone who works here. My mom is constantly befriending salespeople.

"What do you think of this?" Tom asks me. He's

abandoned his chair and his magazine, and now he's holding up a shampoo bottle that says "Man Mane—Make Your Hair Luxuriously Sexy and Touchable." There's a picture of an older man with a full head of hair smiling widely on the bottle. Besides the obvious fact that it's very disgusting to think of my stepfather wanting to be sexy, Tom is almost completely bald. I think maybe he should be concentrating on getting his hair *back*, rather than trying to make the few wisps he has luxurious.

"Why do you need new shampoo?" I ask.

"It's on sale," he says cheerfully, as if that explains it.

"Well, good idea," I say. He opens the bottle and takes a sniff. A little bit of shampoo ends up on his nose.

"Uh-oh," he says, wiping it away with his hand. "Good thing I was planning on buying this." He wanders back over to the shampoos, mumbling something about "You break it, you buy it."

"Samantha!" my mom calls, waving me over to where she's standing with the blond woman. I trudge over reluctantly.

"This is my daughter Samantha," she says to the woman standing next to her. Great. Now my mom is introducing me to the employees by name. I prefer my humiliation to be anonymous, please. "Samantha, this is Joan Clydell. She has a daughter who just started seventh grade, like you."

"Nice to meet you," I say politely. And then I realize Joan isn't a saleswoman, but another shopper who my mom has randomly started speaking to. We've been in the salon about fifteen minutes, and already she's met someone. She probably thinks they're going to be BFFs. Actually, my mom could use a friend her own age. Her best friend, Bibsy, just had a baby, so she's not around as much, and her other best friend, her sister Joanne, moved to Texas so she could start her own cattle ranch. (Total family scandal.)

"Nice to meet you, Samantha," Joan says, giving me a big smile. Hmm. Her teeth have that fake look to them, you know, like the celebs have? I wonder if they hurt. "Let me just find my daughter; I'm sure you'd love to meet her."

Not really. "Of course!" I say brightly. "Um, but Mom, we have to pay for my, um . . ." Somehow saying "eyebrow waxing" sounds kind of gross. Waxing should not be talked about. At all. ". . . My *procedure*." Hmm. Somehow "procedure" sounds even worse. Like something medical or disgusting.

"Oh, fine, fine," my mom says. "Don't worry, I'll take care of it."

"Emma!" Joan Clydell is now yelling her daughter's name into the salon, where a bunch of people are getting their hair cut. "Emma, over here!"

And that's when the red-haired girl from this morning shows up! Little Miss Pink Beret is Joan's daughter! She comes running into the lobby, her newly cut hair shining and bouncing behind her. I should have known her mother would have fake Hollywood teeth.

"Come and meet Samantha. She's in your grade at school," Joan says. Why do mothers always assume that if someone is in your grade at school, that automatically makes you friends? I'm expecting Emma to snub her nose at me, but to my surprise, she shoots me a huge smile.

"Nice to meet you," she says. She looks like she got her hair straightened. Or maybe it's just the way it's been blow-dried. Either way, she looks like a model. I wiggle my new eyebrows at her to keep up.

"Nice to meet you, too," I say, narrowing my eyes. She's obviously putting on a show for the moms. Two can play at this game.

"Did you have a good first day of school?" she asks.

"Not bad," I lie. The moms have moved on, and are now talking about something else. Tax rates in our school district, I think. Does the fact that I make money on my secret-passing business mean I'm going to have to pay taxes? I didn't last year. Am I going to jail? My dad's in finance, so that would be super embarrassing for the whole family, especially since I'm about to be in *You Girl* and everything.

"That's good," Emma says. She surveys the rows of nail polishes that are on the side rack across from the shampoos. She pulls out one that's called Plum Dusk. "What do you think of this one?"

"Um, cute?" I hate when people ask me what I think about something. I never know what to say, since it's always a trick. They either want you to gush about how great whatever they're asking about is, or they want you to commiserate about how bad it is.

"*Totally* cute," she says, putting it in my hand.

"Oh," I say. "You mean do I think it's cute for me?"

"Of course," she says. "I can't wear purple, it clashes with my hair." She sighs, pops the top off the nail polish, and paints my pinky nail. Right there in the store! With a nail polish that's not even hers. Then she pulls me over to the mirror and holds up my hand. "See?" And she's right. With my new eyebrows and my new nails, I look fab. "Don't you love it?"

"Yes." And I do. I do love it. I concentrate on conveying this with my eyebrows.

She smiles and looks pleased. This is turning into a

very weird day. Getting waxed. Buying nail polish with a girl who was super mean to me just hours ago.

Emma looks over at the moms. "My mom talks to every random person she meets. It's sooo embarrassing." She rolls her eyes. Her eyelashes are so light you can hardly even see them. She's dusted them with sparkle powder, so it looks like little flecks of glitter are hovering around her eyes.

"Mine does too," I say.

She looks at me. "Are you really going to be in *You Girl*?"

"Yup," I say. "I'm going over to the photo shoot right after this."

"I love that magazine. Did you see the feature they did on Miley Cyrus last month?" She pulls a round brush off the rack and runs her fingers over the bristles.

"Yeah."

"Do you think you'll get to meet her?"

"Maybe." It's not exactly a lie. I mean, I could *technically* maybe meet her. They didn't really say anything about getting to meet celebs at the photo shoot, but there might be some hanging around. Not Miley, of course, since she was already in the magazine, but maybe someone else. Like maybe the cast of *Twilight*.

"Oh my God, that is so cool," Emma says. She leans

in closer to me, and I can smell the shampoo on her hair. "Hey, do you want to sit with me and Charlie tomorrow at lunch?"

"Sure," I say, shrugging.

"Oh my God." Emma grabs my arm. "Look at that guy!" She collapses into giggles and I look where she's pointing. To my horror, I see Tom over by the shampoos, where Jemima is now helping him pick one out. "I hope that's hair-replenishing shampoo. How embarrassing," Emma says.

"Totally," I agree, grabbing her hand and pulling her back toward the rack of hairbrushes. "What do you think of this one?" I grab the closest thing to me, a black plastic comb. "Um, no," Emma says, looking confused. "Only if you're, like, forty. And a man."

"There she is!" Tom's voice says from behind me. "There's my stepdaughter Samantha. She knows about these kinds of things."

Emma looks at me. "You know that guy?"

"Um, not really, that's just—"

My mom pokes her head around the rack of combs. "Samantha! There you are!" She sounds perturbed. "Is it true you agreed to buy a *twenty-five dollar* eyebrow pencil? That's a bit ridiculous, don't you think?"

I sigh. So much for being cool.

three

"BEAUTIFUL, CANDACE," JAVIER, THE PHOTOG-
rapher, is saying, clicking his camera. "Gorgeous!" In
front of the camera, Candace smiles and blows a kiss
to Javier. Candace is the girl who won *You Girl's* Young
Entrepreneur of the Year award last year, the one who
made bracelets (they're called "peace bracelets," she
told me when I got here) and raised all that money for
Darfur. She's trying to "bring attention to the genocide
that has left more than 200,000 dead from violence and
disease in this region of Africa and aid in the effort to
stop this tragedy through knowledge, monetary aid,
and international intervention." I did *not* know she was
going to be here. Apparently they're doing a "Where is
she now?" segment on her. *And* she gets to come to the
You Girl banquet and give a speech before she hands

over her title. Kind of like Miss America or something.

"Do you think we're going to have pose like that?" the girl sitting next to me on Javier's cream-colored couch asks. Her name's Nikki, and she's here because she runs some kind of website-building company. In front of the camera, Candace smiles and blows another kiss to Javier.

"I hope not," I say.

I thought a photo shoot for a national magazine would be glamorous, but so far all I've been doing is sitting on this couch with Nikki while we watch Candace get her picture taken. Even though there are twenty-five finalists, it's just the three of us here. Nikki lives in New Jersey, and Candace lives in Manhattan, so it makes sense that we'd all get our pictures taken together at a central location.

Javier's studio is right in midtown, about three blocks from where the train from Stamford dropped me off at Grand Central. My sister, Taylor, met me at the train station in Stamford, because apparently my parents decided I'm not old enough to ride the train by myself. Taylor is seventeen. She is also not much of a chaperone, since she spent the whole forty-five-minute train ride talking on the phone with her friend Amanda about some homecoming princess scandal. Then, when we got off the train, she continued to talk on the phone for the whole walk to the studio. And finally, once we got here, she plopped herself down on a chair in the lobby and motioned for me to go ahead. She didn't even take the time to enjoy the midtown crowds. I know you're supposed to hate the crowds in New York, but I love them. The smells, the sounds, the people, all the honking. There's an air of excitement that you definitely don't get in Connecticut.

"I definitely *cannot* pose like that," Nikki says now, watching as Candace pouts at the camera seductively. Geez. For someone who's interested in Darfur, Candace is definitely being a little, uh, suggestive. She's also wearing boots that I'm pretty sure are Gucci. I'm also pretty sure that for the money she spent on those Gucci boots, she could have probably done a lot of good in Darfur.

"I'm sure it'll be okay," I tell Nikki. "As long as you smile, you should be fine."

"Thanks," Nikki says, then frowns. "Um, your eyebrow is—"

But before she can finish her sentence, Javier's assistant, M (seriously, that's her name, just M—when I asked her what it stood for, she gave me a totally weird look, like, *Duh, it's just M*), comes running over, her stilettos clacking on the marble floor. She's all in a panic. "What is going on with your eyebrows?" she demands.

M already wants to kill me because I keep asking her for water. On account of the fact that it's so hot. And all the makeup they've slapped on me is running off my face. I know this because I can feel it, and because M keeps saying, "Ewww, her makeup is running off her face!" in between bringing me plastic cups of warm water.

"Oh," I say, pleased that she's noticed my new brows. "I just got them done. *Professionally*." M could use a trip to the salon herself, if you ask me. Her eyebrows are very thin, like two strands of spaghetti.

"Well, they're dripping off of you," she says, throwing her hands up in the air. Then she produces a mirror from her pocket and shows me my reflection. She's right. The sweat from being in the hot studio is making my eyebrows melt off. Well, not *literally* melt off. More like the eyebrow pencil is melting, leaving a black line down the side of my face. M pulls an eyebrow pencil out of the air and starts fleshing my eyebrows back in.

"Samantha!" Javier calls. "We're ready for you."

"That was fun," Candace says, slipping by me. She's practically skipping. She flops down on the cream-colored couch and slides her legs (and Gucci boots) out in front of her. "Your turn, Secret Agent." Candace thinks it's super witty and fun to call me "Secret Agent" after I told her what my business was. She's not saying it in a nice way, either, but in more of a "I can't believe you pass secrets and I'm trying to save a country and we're somehow both in this room" kind of way. I considered calling her "Darfur Girl" but that doesn't really work, now, does it?

"Good luck," Nikki says. She gives my shoulder a squeeze.

I step over to the chair that's set up in front of a gray backdrop.

"Now, just be natural," Javier instructs. He holds up the camera and takes a shot.

"Oh!" I say, surprised. "Sorry, I wasn't ready." I sit down in the chair, relax my face and give him my most natural-looking smile.

"Over here, Samantha!" Javier instructs. "Look at the camera." Oopsies. I try to look right at the camera, but every time the flash goes off, I blink. So then M comes over and moves my head over to the side, in a very uncomfortable position that I guess is supposed to look good on film, but feels like my head is going to pop off my neck. I try to smile, even though I feel like killing someone.

I try to lean over the way Candace did. I even throw a kiss to the camera. But Javier doesn't say "beautiful" or "fabulous" or anything even remotely resembling positive feedback. He doesn't really say anything except

"Move to the right" and "Stop doing that" and "What are you doing with your lips?" when I try to blow the kiss.

"Okay, okay," he says fifteen minutes later. He sighs and runs his fingers through his dark hair. "Let's take a break, shall we?"

"Good idea," I say, relieved. Until I realize that probably the reason he wants to take a break is because I'm messing up. I step out from under the lights and fan myself with my hand. Why do they keep it so hot in here? They should totally have a fan or something, to blow air at us to cool us off. And give us that cute hair-in-the-wind look. I catch Nikki watching me from the couch near the wall, and I wave her over. Candace is still lounging on the couch, sipping a Red Bull Sugarfree and looking cool as a cucumber.

"Can you tell what I'm doing wrong?" I ask Nikki. "They don't seem to be too pleased with my progress." I catch a glimpse of Javier over toward the side of the room. He and M are having a huddled discussion. Every so often one of them looks over at me. I think I catch one of them saying "hopeless," but I can't be sure.

"Hmmm," Nikki says, following my eyes to the little conference in the corner. "I'm not sure. Maybe you should try not to smile like that."

"Like what?" I ask, my hands flying to my face.

"Like . . . stiff."

Hmm. I practice trying to relax my face. Smile. Frown. Smile. Frown. Smile.

"Also, why do you keep touching your face?"

"I'm afraid my eyebrows are going to melt," I confess.

"Don't worry," Nikki says. "They're fine." She pulls a lip liner out of her purse. "And maybe this will help with the smile." She starts smearing it on my lips.

"I don't think anything's going to help," I say sadly as she works. "I'm not trying to smile weird. I always have problems with getting my picture taken." I look around nervously. M is not going to be pleased about the lip liner, especially since I already gave her a little bit of grief about the makeup. After she'd caked a bunch on me, I said, "I think I have enough makeup on now," and she rolled her eyes and told me that when they finally did the shoot, it would look like I had nothing on at all. I guess it has to do with stage makeup, like how actors wear a ton, but when you're watching TV, you can't tell. Even so, my face feels like it's going to fall off.

"Hold still," Nikki instructs. "I'm trying to make your lips go up a little bit at the ends, so that it looks like you're smiling normally."

"Thankth," I say around the lip liner. "But won't it make my lips too red?"

"What would you rather have the nation seeing?" Nikki says. "Red lips or a weird smile?"

"Red lips," I say. But I'm not sure. I wish my mom was here, so that I could get a second opinion. Or even Taylor. But my mom had to work the night shift (she's a nurse, and so she's always working crazy hours). And of course Taylor's in the lobby, probably texting about the homecoming crisis. Figures I'd be abandoned in my time of need.

"There," Nikki says. She holds out the tissue. "Blot," she instructs. I blot my lips on the tissue. "Now take a sip of this." She holds out a bottle of water with a straw in it, and I take a few sips. The cold liquid feels sweet and good on my throat. I can feel little beads of sweat starting to pool around my forehead. I hope those won't show up on film.

"Are we ready?" Javier asks, clapping his hands and walking back over to where I'm sitting. He looks annoyed. Probably he wants to get home to his family. Nikki scurries back over to the side of the room.

"Is this the longest photo shoot you've ever done?" I ask him, trying to lighten the mood. I concentrate on trying to keep my head in the position M put me in. I smile and wiggle my eyebrows. Then I lean over and tilt my face toward the camera.

"No," he says. *Click, click.* My eyes are watering from the flash, but I force myself to keep them open. "Some celebrities insist I shoot them over and over again until I get it right."

"Wow," I say. "You've shot celebrities?" Wait until I tell Emma I had a celebrity photographer! How fab! I stand up and put my hands on my hips, looking right into the camera.

"What's all over your mouth?" M asks. She looks panicked, like she's just been called down to the principal's office or something. She grabs a tissue out of her pocket.

"It's lip liner," I say, turning my head away so that she won't try to wipe it off my lips. I've definitely decided that I would much rather have red lips than have a weird-looking smile on my face.

"It's okay," Javier says, snapping away. "It will look good on film and even out the smile. Whoever did that is a genius, love."

I shoot a grateful smile to Nikki, and she gives me a thumbs-up. I twist and turn and smile and jut my hip and sit and stand and listen to everything Javier is telling me to do.

"That's a wrap on Samantha," Javier says a little while later.

I'm exhausted. And I think I sprained my ankle trying

to do one of the poses. "What?" I ask. "Already? Did we get a good one?"

"You did fine," Javier says, motioning to Nikki to take her place in front of the camera. Hmm. That doesn't sound too promising. I don't want to do fine. I want to be fabulous, glamorous, and wonderful. But I guess that's hard to do when you're wearing pink Skechers and not Gucci boots. Plus I suppose I'll have to settle for it, since M is ushering me out from in front of the camera and over toward the door.

"Good luck," I say to Nikki as I breeze by her.

"Thanks," she says, taking her place in front of the camera.

"Later, Secret Agent," Candace says. She's texting someone on her phone. I don't think people in Darfur can afford cell phones. Shouldn't she be abstaining if she's so worried about them? And why is she hanging around? Isn't her photo shoot over?

"Oh, good," Taylor says when I get to the lobby. She slaps her phone shut. "You're finished. What's all over your lips?"

"Lip liner." I don't bother mentioning that the reason I'm wearing it is because I'm the most unphotogenic person, like, ever. And then I have a thought. "Hey, Taylor," I say excitedly. "Do you think they're going to airbrush me? Like they do with all the top models?"

"I doubt they airbrush in the tween mags." Taylor rolls her brown eyes, like tween mags are about as relevant as iPods without video screens.

She then proceeds to spend the whole train ride back to Stamford on the phone with her boyfriend. His name is Ryan, and he is very, very cute. Last year I kind of sort of had this crush on him, because whenever he came over, he would watch the Disney Channel with me while he waited for Taylor to get ready for wherever they were going.

If I had a little sister, and Jake was my boyfriend, I wonder if he'd watch the Disney Channel with her while I got ready for our dates. I'd be up in my room, drying my hair and trying on five different outfits, and he'd be downstairs, totally pretending to be into the latest Disney shows. And of course he wouldn't really *want* to watch Disney, but he'd know it was a nice thing to do for my sister, so he would. Thinking of Jake taking me on a date makes my face start to feel hot, so I press it against the window of the train so Taylor doesn't notice.

When our train pulls in, my dad's car is waiting for us right outside the station.

"How was it?" he asks as we pile in. He slides his BlackBerry into his shirt pocket. My dad is always on his phone after hours, since he works with a lot of stocks and things, and the markets are open in other places when they're not open here, because there are time differences.

"It was fun," I say, settling into the backseat and buckling my seat belt. Taylor always gets the front, because she's older. I'm not sure who made that rule. Probably Taylor. She's big on making rules. Especially ones that make no sense.

"And how was the first day of school?" my dad asks, turning his car onto the highway. "Any potential for new business?"

"Loads," I say. "There are so many new kids, it's crazy. Oh, and Daphne made me some posters so I can start advertising."

"That's wonderful," my dad says, "But perhaps you should look into digital media to advertise. Everyone— music companies, television and movie studios—they're all looking to digital and social media as the wave of the future."

"There's a digital media class at school," I say, "Maybe I'll get into it."

"Does anyone care how *my* first day of school went?" Taylor asks, pouting her lips and pretending to be upset. Honestly, the only reason my dad asked me first was because Taylor tends to monopolize conversations. Once you get her going, she won't shut up.

"How was your first day of school, Taylor?" my dad asks. His BlackBerry starts beeping, and he checks the screen and then sends it to voicemail.

"Horrible," Taylor says. "They're going to be voting for homecoming court next week, which gives me no time to campaign." She turns around and looks at me. "Maybe while you're at it, you can see how digital media might help me to win homecoming princess, since Julia Peterson came back from summer vacation with a nose job, and everyone is going to vote for her."

I settle back into my seat and listen to my dad explain to Taylor that she shouldn't *mock* digital media, and how she could launch a web campaign, and how he's sure that Julia Peterson didn't really get a nose job. To which my sister replies, "Trust me, Dad, her nose is, like, an inch shorter." So I decide it's time to pull my iPod out of my bag and listen to music for the rest of the ride home.

I'm so caught up in the music that I don't realize that Tom's outside when my dad pulls up in front of our house to drop me off. He's on the front lawn, raking leaves and wearing a baseball hat.

My dad slows the car to a stop in front of the house, his jaw set in a straight line. He does not turn into the driveway. Taylor, oblivious to the situation, keeps blabbering on about homecoming.

"Thanks for the ride," I say, not mentioning the fact that my dad has refused to pull into the driveway. I start to fumble with my seat belt.

"You can at least wait until he pulls into the driveway, Samantha; I mean, you don't have to be in that much of a—" She trails off as she sees Tom raking in the front yard. His back is to us, sparing me from more of a scene. The thing is, my dad doesn't like Tom. Like, really, *really* doesn't like him. Even though my parents have been divorced for five years, he just hates the idea of my mom being remarried. Weird, right?

"Bye, Dad," I say brightly.

"Bye, Dad," Taylor says. She's out of the car and halfway up the driveway before I'm even done with my seat belt.

"I'll call you tomorrow, sweetheart," my dad says.

I slam the door and run up to the house. I can hear the slight squeal of tires as my dad pulls away.

"Oh, Samantha!" Tom says. "I didn't see you there."

"Really?" I say. "My dad just dropped us off."

"Oh, good," he says. "How was the photo shoot? Must have been interesting, eh?"

"You have no idea," I say, and head into the house to call Daphne.

four

THE NEXT MORNING, EMMA AND CHARLIE
are waiting for me at my locker. Emma's holding one of
the flyers Daphne and I put up yesterday. "Do you really
pass secrets?" she asks.

"Ye-ess," I say slowly. I spin the dial on my locker. I
hope they don't think it's babyish. The secret-passing, I
mean. There are two secrets waiting for me in my locker.
One of the secrets is for Ronald Hughes, the kid from my
elementary school who's crazy. Ronald actually gets a lot
of secrets passed to him—usually they say things like
"Ronald, YOU ARE OUT OF YOUR TREE" and "Ronald,
please return the eraser you took out of my desk" and
"Ronald, I think it would be funny if you farted during
the Presidential Physical Fitness Test in gym today!"

The other secret is for someone named Kayleigh Mills.

I have no idea who that is. Occupational hazard, I suppose, of starting to expand my business. "Hey," I say, "do you guys know who Kayleigh Mills is?"

"Are those the secrets?" Charlie asks, leaning in to get a better look. The tips of her long hair brush against the note. "Who sent that to her?"

"I dunno," I say.

"Let's open it!" Emma says excitedly.

"I can't open them." I clutch the notes closer to me, just in case they try to pry them out of my hands. Wow. I never thought of that. I could totally get secretjacked. Like carjacked, only with secrets.

"You don't open them? Like, ever?" Emma looks shocked.

"No way," I say. "I can't, it would ruin my business."

"How much money do you make?" Charlie asks.

"It depends. This morning I only made two dollars." She looks disappointed. "But last year I was making tons, especially around Valentine's Day."

I spot Ronald heading down the hall in the other direction. "Hey, Ronald!" I yell. "You have a secret."

Ronald grabs the paper out of my hands. "Thanks!" he says as he takes off down the hall.

"You know him?" Emma asks. She raises her perfectly plucked eyebrows. How does she get them like that? They're like two perfect half moons over her eyes. "He's cute."

I almost drop my backpack. Ronald Hughes, *cute*? Is she crazy? Cute makes me think of puppies, or the color pink. Ronald Hughes is definitely not cute. Disturbing, maybe. Weird, even. Maybe kind of crazy on a good day. But definitely not cute. Wait a minute. Is this one of those things you always see in movies? Where the guys who weren't popular somehow grow up and become virtual girl magnets overnight? Also, why does this never happen to girls? How come I can't grow up and become a virtual boy magnet? Taylor is a boy magnet, but she was always a boy magnet. This seems very unfair.

"Anyway, I think this is a fab idea," Emma says, and Charlie nods. "I mean, you're going to have access to the whole school's gossip and secrets." Her face is getting flushed with excitement. "Samantha! You are totally going to rule the school!"

"Guys, um, it doesn't really work that way," I say nervously. "I can't just go around reading them, that would totally—"

Charlie waves her hand at me. "Of course you would still keep it a secret, even if you read it," she says. "Sometimes it's fun just knowing." A song comes tinkling out of her purse, and she pulls out a small silver and blue cell phone. "Ugh," she says. "It's Mark." She says this like it should be enough of an explanation and then flounces off down the hall.

"Okay, listen," Emma says, once Charlie is out of earshot. "I want to pass a secret." She pulls a tightly folded piece of paper out of her binder. There's a dollar clipped to the top.

"Cool," I say, reaching for it. But she pulls it out of my reach.

"Now, listen," she says, "I want to make it clear that usually I don't do things like this." She pulls a piece of her long red hair and twirls it around her finger. Then her tone turns serious. "I don't believe in playing mind games." Yikes.

"Okay," I say uncertainly.

"But I think this is a totally cute and fab way to flirt, keep a guy guessing, you know?" She smiles. "So here you go!" She shoves the note in my hand.

I look down at the note in my hand. It says "Jake Giacandi" on the front. Oh. My. God. My heart starts to slide down into my stomach, and I try to stop it by telling myself that this note means nothing. In fact, it probably says something really stupid. For example, maybe Emma wants to ask Jake about what kind of skateboard to buy. But then, how would she know that Jake skateboards? Actually, how would she really know Jake at all? Besides their little chat in homeroom the other day, have they even talked?

I want to ask her what's in the note, but I can't really come out and say that, now, can I? After my whole big spiel about how the secrets are private and anonymous, it probably wouldn't look too good to go around asking her what's in it.

"So when will you give it to him?" Emma asks.

"Um, usually I give all the secrets out after lunch." This isn't totally true. In fact it's pretty much a complete lie. Usually I just give the secrets to people whenever I see them. But I can't just go give Jake a note from Emma immediately. This is an emergency situation, and I need some time to think about this, so that I can come up with some kind of brilliant plan. A slight delay in the passing of the secret is totally justified. After all, this is a previously unencountered situation. One of those "new business challenges" my dad is always talking about.

"But you just gave Ronald his secret, and it's the morning," Emma points out. She flips her long hair over her shoulder and narrows her eyes at me. The look on her face reminds me of yesterday when she saw I was in her seat.

"True," I say. "But that's only because I wanted to get

it over with. Ronald's crazy." Emma looks at me skeptically, so I twirl my finger around by my ear to kind of drive the point home. "Totally crazy. One time last year he stole our teacher's coat and wore it out on the playground."

Emma wrinkles her nose. "Weird," she says.

"Yeah," I agree. "It was this really long black fur thing that he kept tripping over. He wanted to take the teacher's snow boots, too, but he couldn't get them out of the classroom without getting caught."

"Well, anyway," Emma says. She's looking at me strangely. I'm pretty sure she didn't buy that whole coat story, even though it's true. "Can you just let me know when you give it to Jake? I really want to see his reaction, you know, like if he acts different around me once he gets the note."

If he acts different around her once he gets the note? Is she crazy? She's only known him for one day! How can he possibly act different around her? She doesn't have anything to compare it to. Not like me. I have tons and tons of Jake memories. And not just TSSI, either. I have the time that we Photoshopped Daphne's head onto a picture of a clown for her birthday party invitations in fifth grade. And the time Jake came over to my house for dinner and he ate four whole corn on the cobs, and my mom and Tom couldn't believe it, and they totally thought we were hiding the corn somewhere. Or the time that I went with Jake's family to the water park, and I got completely drenched by this really big wave and Jake and his brothers said I looked like a drowned rat.

And okay, fine, maybe those aren't the most romantic memories ever (especially that last one—I mean, a drowned rat isn't exactly a compliment), but that's not the point! The point *is*, if *I* told Jake I liked him, if *I* was the one who was sending him a note, *I* would have something to compare it to. *I* would know if he suddenly got weird and didn't want to eat four corn on the cobs in front of me, or if he wasn't calling me a drowned rat and was instead trying to help me dry off at the water park, that then things would have changed.

But Emma. How could *she* tell? They have no history!

But I don't say that. Because I can't.

So I just slip the note into my bag and say, "Of course I'll let you know."

And then the bell rings and we head to homeroom.

That note taunts me all morning. It stares up at me from my book bag, laughing and pointing. It's almost enough to make me regret the way I begged my mom for the bag I wanted—a very cute tan suede that is sophisticated and cool, but is not a normal book bag. It's one of those bags with an open top. So all through the day, every time I look down, I can SEE THAT NOTE.

It taunts me all through English.

It taunts me all through science.

It taunts me all through study hall, which is the worst because I have nothing to keep my mind on, and at one point I honestly think the note might have actually screamed, *"OPEN ME RIGHT NOW, SAMANTHA, YOU KNOW YOU WANT TO READ ME!"*

"I'm dying," I say to Daphne at lunch. "I. AM. DYING."

Daphne reaches her hand out and touches my forehead. "You don't have a fever," she says.

"I'm not *sick*," I say. I reach into my bag and pull out the tuna fish sandwich my mom packed me this morning. I look around the middle school cafeteria. This place is so *confusing*. Last year, it was super simple. You ate with your class, and that was it. Now there are, like, *tables* of people all, you know, *mixed-up*. "It was an expression."

I pull the secret out of my bag and drop it on the table. "Look at that," I say to Daphne.

"Looks like a piece of paper," she says.

"Not just a piece of paper," I tell her. "It's a secret. And do you know whose name is on that secret?"

Daphne picks it up and looks at it. "It's for Jake," she says.

"Yes! And do you know who it's from?"

"No," Daphne says.

"It's from Emma! Emma is sending secrets to Jake!"

"No!" Daphne shrieks. She grabs the paper out of my hand and waves it around. "Why would she *do* that?" This is why Daphne and I are BFFs. She hasn't even met Emma. All she knows is what I told her when I called her last night to fill her in on all things *You Girl*, Emma, and eyebrows. But she already understands just how completely severe the situation is.

"Why do you think?" I say. "She probably loves him." I take a bite of my tuna fish sandwich. Ugh. Totally soggy. My mom really has to stop letting Tom make the sandwiches. She knows he has a trigger finger with the mayo.

"That little brat," Daphne says. "She thinks she can just step in and LOVE HIM AFTER ONE DAY?"

"That's what I thought!" See? Perfect BFFs!

"You have to read it," Daphne says. She's holding the paper up to the light, trying to see through it.

"Don't do that," I say, snatching it away from her. "Someone could see." I look around the cafeteria to make sure no one's noticed. But no one has. In fact, it's kind of like we're invisible. Sigh. I know I should put the note back in my bag before something *untoward* happens to it. But I can't! It's like if I let it out of my sight, something horrible will happen.

"You have to read it," Daphne says again.

"I can't *read* it," I say. "That would be compromising the integrity of my entire business."

"But if you don't read it," Daphne says, "you'll be compromising the integrity of your entire romantic future."

"Well . . . when you put it that way." I stare at the paper, which is folded up nice and neat. JAKE GIACANDI is written on the front in sparkly gold gel pen. "Maybe I could just open it up, read it, and then tape it back up."

"Good idea!" Daphne says. She sounds excited. "You can totally read it, and then tape it back up!"

"I don't have any tape, though," I say. Maybe I could just accidentally on purpose lose it. That happens, right? Even the U.S. Postal Service loses things once in a while. I know because my grandparents are always complaining about it.

"This is a school," Daphne says. She rolls her eyes. "I'm sure if you needed to find some tape, you could." Good point.

I start to pull the top of one edge of the paper down

just a tiny, tiny bit. "Wait!" I scream. Two guys from the table behind us turn to look.

"Who are you talking to?" Daphne frowns. "You're the one holding the note."

"What if it says something I don't want to know?" I ask her. "Then what?"

"What would you not want to know?" Daphne asks. She takes a sip of her juice box and then looks at it sadly. "I don't think I'm going to be able to bring juice boxes to school anymore," she says. "No one else has a juice box."

"I mean, I don't know *for sure* that it says she likes him," I say. "And if I read it, and it *does* say that, it would be like opening up a huge can of worms."

"But that's exactly why you need to open it," Daphne says. "You need to know for sure."

"Maybe," I say, deciding to abandon reason and go back to my earlier theory, "it's something totally innocent, like how she wants him to give her skateboarding tips or something."

Daphne frowns. "Um, Samantha? Does Emma look like the kind of girl who skateboards?"

I look across the cafeteria to where Emma is waiting in line for her hot lunch. She's sipping out of a Diet Coke can with one hand, and texting someone covertly on her cell with the other. As she does so, her silver charm bracelet jangles down her arm.

"Not really," I say. "But maybe her brother or something—"

"What did she say," Daphne asks, "right before she gave you the note?"

"Um, she said that she didn't usually do this, that she wasn't usually into games, but that"—I swallow—"but that she thought the secret-passing thing was a cute way to flirt."

Daphne doesn't say anything, she just gets really busy putting her empty juice box back into her bag. "You should open it," she says. "I mean, these are dire circumstances. If she likes Jake—and let's be honest, it sounds like she does—then you have to know."

"Why, though?" Denial sounds kind of fun right about now.

"So that you can do something about it! Go after him, tell Jake how you feel!"

"Yeah, right," I say. I trace my fingers over the writing on the front of the purple paper. *J. A. K. E.* in swirly letters. God, this is annoying. I mean, why is EMMA writing his name in swirly script, like, with LOVE or something, when *I* am the one who has known him forever? She thinks she can just come waltzing into . . . I don't know, *here* or something, and just take over? *I'm* the one who's been watching Jake skateboard since forever. *I'm* the one who shared a moment with him right before he went to camp, and *I'm* the one who's been writing him all summer, trying to keep his spirits up! Well, a few postcards. But that's better than the none that Emma wrote him!

"You're right," I say to Daphne. "I have a right to open up this note!"

"Do it!" Daphne cries.

I am like a soldier going off to battle. I set the note slowly down on my binder. Then, very carefully, so that I can maybe seal it up later if I want to, I slide my finger under the tape that's holding the note together. It catches on the side of my finger, so I apply a little more pressure. Just a little more, a littttlllee morrrreee . . . The tape starts to tear on the side, and I'm just about to break through, just about to see what's in this super secret note, just about to learn the truth about—

"There you are!" Emma says from behind me, and I scream and drop the note on the floor.

"Wow, you don't have to, like, freak out about it," she says. She sits down next to me and flips her long red hair over her shoulder. "Anyway," she says, "I have major news."

"Oh, really?" I say. Her secret note is on the ground, and obviously it won't do to have her see it, because then she's going to be all, *Um, why is my note on the ground when I specifically asked you to give it to Jake?* So I quickly cover it with my foot.

"Yes," she says. "Major news." She looks over to where Charlie is still standing in line, looking at some yogurt. "Ugh," she says. "I really wish she'd get over here." We watch as Charlie pulls the tab off a container of yogurt, slips a plastic spoon in, and takes a small bite. Then she makes a disgusted face and drops it in the trash. The lunch lady behind the yogurt bar looks at her and then patiently hands her another kind.

"What's she doing?" Daphne asks.

"She has weird food allergies," Emma says. "It's like acid reflux or something, way gross."

"But why is she taking one bite of a yogurt and then throwing the rest out?" I ask. I watch as another container goes plopping into the trash.

"She has to figure out which ones she can eat," Emma says. "She knows from tasting them if she can handle a whole container or not."

I want to ask why Charlie doesn't just bring her own yogurt from home, or why she doesn't know what brands she can eat, but Charlie's weird acid reflux stuff is completely forgotten by what Emma tells me next.

"Okay, so brace yourself," she tells me. "This news isn't good."

"What news isn't good?" I ask warily. But then I perk up a little. Maybe she's going to say that she told Jake that she liked him, and he rejected her. Maybe he told her that he likes someone else, someone he's known forever, someone with really cute eyebrows. Maybe Emma decided she didn't really want to—

"Who are you?" Emma suddenly demands, looking across the table at Daphne.

"Oh," Daphne says. "I'm Daphne." She holds her hand over the table, but Emma looks at her suspiciously.

"Can she be trusted?" she asks me.

"Who?" I ask. "*Daphne?*"

"Yes, *her*," Emma says, looking at Daphne with distaste.

"Um, yeah," I say. "She can be trusted."

"Okay," she says. "Well, then." She pauses and then looks around the cafeteria dramatically. She reaches into her big black leather bag and pulls out a wrinkled-up piece of paper. "I found this on the wall outside of our homeroom."

I look down at it. It's light yellow, with an aqua trim, and here's what it says:

DO YOU HAVE A SECRET YOU'RE JUST DYING TO TELL?

Get into the 21st century and send your secret to Olivia@tellmeasecretmillboro.com and I'll pass it on to whoever you want. Don't take the chance that your secret could fall into the wrong hands! Would you want your secret to be known all over school if one of those other secret-passers loses it, or drops it, or something?

I don't think so!

Use our secure online payment form at tellmeasecretmillboro.com or prepay for your secret by dropping a dollar into locker 245. Be sure to include your name! For our first week, buy one get one free!

XXO,

Olivia

P.S. If you want to be all old-fashioned about it, I will accept handwritten secrets in my locker, too, number 245.

For a second, I just stare at the paper, sure this has to be a joke. I mean, who does that? Just steals someone's idea for a business? Not to mention this flyer isn't very professional. There are tons of run-on sentences, it doesn't really have a structure, and it's very confusing. Plus what does she mean by "those other secret-passers"? Everyone knows I'm the only other secret-passer around these parts.

"Where did you get this?" I ask.

"I told you," Emma says. "It was on the wall outside our homeroom."

"Did you see any other ones?"

"Yes." She takes a dainty sip of her milk. "But don't worry, I took care of them." She opens up her bag, and at the bottom, all scrunched up, are dozens and dozens of the same light yellow papers. I look at her, shocked.

"You took them all down?" I ask, dazed.

"Yes," Emma says.

"Good for you," Daphne says. "Honestly, that's so stupid, stealing someone's idea for a business."

Emma looks at her sharply. "What's your name again?" she asks.

"Daphne," Daphne says, sighing.

"Well, *Daph*ne, all I know is that someone close to Samantha's business might have been leaking top-level secrets about how it's run." She looks at me. "It's important that in business, we can trust our advisers."

"Daphne's not my adviser," I say, rolling my eyes. "And she doesn't know any top-level secrets, there *are* no top-level secrets about how I run my business; I just do it. You put the secret in the locker and I pass it, easy as that."

"Yeah," Daphne says. She looks really cranky.

"Oh," Emma says. "Sorry." She gives us both a winning smile. "Now, this total travesty we've just encountered can call for only one thing."

"What's that?" I ask.

"A sleepover," she says. "To plan on how to take Olivia DOWN." She claps her hands excitedly.

"Hmmm," I say. "A sleepover." To be totally honest, I don't love sleepovers the way some people do. Don't get me wrong, there's nothing, like, *bad* about sleepovers. I'm all for the having-fun part, and the gorging-yourself-on-pizza part, and the doing-makeovers part. But I like to have people over to *my* house, because I do sometimes, just once in a while, get nervous sleeping other places. But only once in a while. And only certain places. I'm totally fine sleeping at Daphne's, for example. "I could probably ask if I could have everyone over at my house," I say.

"Sleepovers are always at Emma's house," Charlie says. She's at our table now, and sets her tray down next to Daphne's lunch bag. It contains one container of blueberry yogurt and five wrapped-up, low-fat cheese sticks. Hmm. Weird. I don't think Daphne needs to be too worried. One juice box probably isn't going to stick out in this crowd.

Emma nods. "They are," she says, and doesn't offer any other information—like, for example, *why* sleepovers are always at her house. "So tonight. Seven o'clock. Be there." She looks across the table at Daphne. "You'd better come too."

"Thanks," Daphne says. "Sounds great." She kicks me under the table, like, *"Hello, why the heck would we go over to her house, especially if she likes Jake, duh."*

"Look," I try. "I'm going to need to ask my mom if—"

"Samantha," Emma says, sighing. "That's fine, but if I were you, I'd be there. How can we stop this if we don't have a plan?"

"I don't know," I say.

"Ugh, this yogurt is definitely not agreeing with my stomach," Charlie says. She sets it down on her tray. "Why don't they have Fage here like every other place?"

"You should get your mom to write a note," Emma says. "Like, protesting the food or something."

"Totally." Charlie dumps her spoon back into her yogurt and pushes her tray away from her. Her cheese sticks go untouched. She picks up one of Olivia's flyers. "So what's the deal?" she asks, waving it. "With this?"

"The deal," Emma says, "is that someone is starting the exact same business as Samantha. I told you that in math."

"It doesn't seem, like, exactly the same," Charlie says, her eyes scanning down the page. "It seems like this one is virtual."

"Virtual?" I ask.

"Yeah, like on the internet, digital, you know, the wave of the future." Charlie pushes her chair back and looks around the cafeteria, bored. "I really wish Mark was in this lunch period."

I still don't know who Mark is, and I'm about to maybe ask her, just in case he has a cute friend Emma can get hooked up with so that she will stop thinking about Jake, when I remember what my dad said to me yesterday about everything going digital nowadays, and I feel my stomach do a flip.

"Ooh, that reminds me," Emma says. "Did you give my note to Jake yet?"

Daphne and I look at each other across the lunch table. "Um, not yet," I say. "But I will as soon as I see him."

When lunch is over, and Emma and Charlie have taken off for their art class, I reach down and carefully slide the note up from under the table and back into my bag. Middle school so far? Um, pretty much a disaster.

five

WHAT DOES ONE BRING TO A sleepover at the house of the-most-popular-girl-in-school-who-might-like-your-crush when one is trying to make a good impression? You'd think it wouldn't be that hard to figure out, right? You throw some pajamas and a toothbrush in a bag, and you're good to go.

But on the way out of school, while I was walking to my bus, I ran into Emma and she said, "See you tonight, I'll text you the address. And don't forget to bring a karaoke outfit!" Then she kissed me on both cheeks(!!) and was gone.

A karaoke outfit? I have no clue *what* she is talking about.

So now I'm home, and I have pulled every single thing out of my closet, including all my bags, because now even my tote bags don't look right. I mean, I can't exactly show up at Emma's house with all my stuff in a "I ♡ Cheese" duffel, can I? (In my defense, it's not even mine. Tom got it at some kind of food show he went to when he was working in the food industry. Tom's had a lot of different jobs. He works at the phone company now, although I'm not exactly sure what he does there.)

I survey the mess in front of me and decide there's only one thing to do.

"Taylor!" I scream. "I need you!"

"What?" she rushes into my room, her cell phone to her ear. "What is it *now*?" Wow. That's really not very friendly. And what does she mean by "now"? I hardly ever ask Taylor for help. Only, like, once a week. Or maybe twice or three times.

"I need help packing for my sleepover," I say.

"Oh." She tells whoever's on the phone she has to go, then slaps the phone shut. She looks at the big jumble of clothes, shoes, and bags that's littering the bedroom floor.

"It's not my faulllltttt," I whine before she can say anything. "I don't know what to brinnnngg."

"To Daphne's?" Taylor asks. "You go there all the time."

"No, to Emma's."

"Who's Emma?"

"Emma is this girl who goes to my school, she went to

Kennedy, and she's very popular and very cool and she has long red curly hair and she's having a sleepover and she said to bring a karaoke outfit do you EVEN KNOW WHAT THAT MEANS?" Wow. I'm really starting to get myself all worked up, which I don't think is good for my skin. Or my eyebrows. Also, I hope the fact that Emma might like Jake isn't important when it comes to my fashion choices. I cannot tell Taylor about that situation, because Taylor doesn't even know that *I* like Jake. The only person who knows about *that* is Daphne.

"First of all, you need to calm down," Taylor says. "You're freaking out." Her hands are flying over her phone, texting away. Probably to the person she just hung up with. Which was probably Ryan. They're usually in constant contact.

"Okay," I say, sitting down on my bed. I don't feel so good. I wonder if maybe I should put my head between my legs or something, like I had to do that time I broke my wrist and almost fainted at the hospital.

"Now," Taylor says. "You cannot bring that 'I heart cheese' bag; that's just offensive."

"Cheese is offensive?"

"No, bringing that bag to someone's house is offensive. It's like you're saying you don't care about their opinion one little bit."

"Agreed," I say. Even *I* knew that bag wasn't going to cut it. And I kind of hate cheese. Although Charlie might have liked it; she had all those cheese sticks on her tray today.

"You can borrow my purple Adidas bag," she says. "It's cute, but casual, so it won't look like you're trying too hard."

This is why I love my sister! Honestly, she can be cranky and annoying and sometimes she's self-absorbed, but when it comes down to it, who else would get the importance of a purple Adidas tote bag in a situation like this?

Twenty minutes later, I'm all packed up. Taylor has lent me not only her bag, but also these really cute pajamas (Her: "If you spill anything on them, I will kill you!" Me: "All eating will be done before I change into my pajamas, promise!") that consist of a pink and white shirt and soft cotton pants with hearts all over them. I'm wearing jeans and a red sweater over to Emma's, and for my karaoke outfit, which Taylor had to explain to me ("No, I don't think it means you're going out to do karaoke, they only do that in bars, you're thirteen—it probably means you're going to do karaoke at her house and she wants you to dress up like a rock star"), she lent me a really cute short silver dress with beading up and down the skirt, black footless tights, and matching silver ballet flats.

Taylor has gone back to her room and is on the phone again (I can hear her laughter coming through the wall that separates her room from mine), and I am waiting for Tom to get home from work so that he can drive me and Daphne to Emma's.

What should I do for the next half hour? I could start my homework, I guess. I pull my math book out and look at it forlornly. Honestly, though, who does homework on a Friday night? I'll have all day tomorrow to do it. And Sunday, even.

The doorbell rings, and I hear my mom downstairs opening it.

And then I hear her say, "Well, hello, Jake, how nice to see you. Did you have a nice summer?"

What?! Jake! Jake is here! Jake is here, in my house! For the love of God, Jake has come over to see me! I rush over to my mirror and run a brush through my hair, then swipe some more lip gloss over my lips. I squeeze my cheeks the way I've seen Taylor's friend Amanda do when she wants to give them some color. I lean over and look closely at my eyebrows, hoping they don't look painted on. They don't. They look great, actually. Thank God for eyebrow pencils! And thank goodness for excellent eyebrow artists, like Jemima. I hope my mom gave her a good tip.

I'm about to rush down the stairs, but then Jake is at my bedroom door.

"Hey," he says.

"Hi," I say. My stomach does the hugest flip ever, and my heart speeds up. Jake's wearing blue mesh shorts and a white Quiksilver T-shirt, and he smiles at me and then flops down on my bed.

"Do you guys want a snack?" my mom yells up from downstairs.

"Do you?" I ask Jake.

"Sure," he says, shrugging.

"Yes, please," I yell back. I hear my mom shuffle back to the kitchen. Apparently she is unfazed by the fact that I have a boy in my room, something she would never let Taylor do in a million years. Of course, Taylor's older than me and has a boyfriend. But still. I'm thirteen! That is definitely old enough to kiss a boy. Unless. Does my mom think that I'm unkissable? Does she think that because Jake has been coming up to my room all the time since we were, like, five that it means he doesn't want to or won't kiss me? Does Jake think that? Is that why he is just sitting on my bed, throwing a nerf basketball in the air like it's nothing? Oh, God, this is confusing.

"What's up?" Jake asks.

"Nothing," I say. "Getting ready to go to a sleepover."

"At Daphne's? You two should hang out with me for a little bit; we could play Guitar Hero or something at my house."

"No, at, uh . . . at another friend's house," I say. I hope he doesn't ask me who.

"Who?"

"Just this girl," I clear my throat. "Um, you know Emma? From our homeroom?" I cross my fingers that he'll say something like *"Oh, her? Ewww, she's not cute at all,"* or *"Wow, that one really fell off the ugly truck,"* or *"Sorry, I haven't noticed anyone in our homeroom besides you, Samantha."*

"The one with the red hair?" he asks.

"Yeah," I say. "Her." I'm sitting next to him on the bed now, but pretty far away. I can't decide what a safe distance is. It has to be far enough so that he doesn't think I like him, but not too far, because that would be weird, and he might start thinking that I'm sitting so far away from him so that I don't tip him off that I like him.

"I didn't know you were friends with Emma," Jake says.

"I'm not," I say quickly. "I mean, we are. Sort of. I guess. She found this"— I pull one of Olivia's flyers out of my backpack and hold it out to him—"and she wants to help me."

Our fingers brush against each other as Jake takes the paper from me, and I try not to faint. Okay, that's a little dramatic. I'm not going to *faint*, obviously. I mean, that would be way crazy. But touching Jake's fingers now is soooo different than before the summer. "Emma's going to help you?" Jake sounds doubtful.

"Yeah," I say. "Well, not just Emma. Her friend Charlie and Daphne are going to be there too. We're all going to brainstorm."

"Oh," he says. He seems like he's about to say something else, like maybe he *wants* to say something else, like maybe he's *thinking* about saying something else, but then he spots something in my book bag.

"What's that?" he asks. I follow his gaze. Right over to where the note that Emma gave me this morning is poking up out of my bag! Darn you, cute, open-topped bag! I really am thinking about trading it in for a normal backpack. "Oh, that's just a secret I'm supposed to pass," I say. It's called downplaying.

"It has my name on it," Jake says.

"Oh, right," I say, breezily, hoping I sound innocent. "It's for you, totally." I pluck the note right out of my bag and then hand it to him. Which I was going to do anyway. Really, I was. I wasn't going to *keep* it from him, that would have been ridiculous, not to mention completely wrong. It would go against everything I stand for, and so—

He's reading it. He's opening the note! Right there in front of me, he is Opening. The. Note. I can't decide what's worse—him opening the note in front of me, or him taking it home and reading it in private. He slides his finger under the tape and then unfolds the paper. He scans it, and I keep my eyes on his face, trying to get any hints as to what it might say. But there's nothing! His face is like a blank piece of paper!

"You don't get many secrets," I try.

"Yeah," he says. He finishes reading the secret, then folds it up carefully and slides it into his pocket. He's keeping it! He's keeping the secret! Does he want to read it over later? Did she confess her love to him? Is he going to tell me what was in the stupid thing?

"So what did—" I start, but my mom appears in the bedroom doorway, her hands full with a package of Oreos and two glasses of milk.

"Here you go," she says, handing each of us a glass of milk and setting the package of Oreos down on the bed in between us.

"Thanks," I say. I tear open the pack of cookies and

pull one out. No use going to Emma's hungry, especially with Charlie's acid reflux problem. Who knows what kind of weird food will be served.

"Oh, and this came for you in the mail," my mom says, handing me a cream-colored envelope. "It's from *You Girl.*"

I tear it open.

You are invited to the
You Girl *Annual Presentation Dinner.*
Please join us at the King Tower Hotel,
New York, NY, for dinner and cocktails as we
announce the winner of the 7th annual
You Girl *Young Entrepreneur of the Year award.*

It's written on gold paper, and two tickets fall out into my hand.

"That's so awesome," Jake says. He dunks a cookie into his milk and takes a bite.

"Congratulations, honey," my mom says. She squeezes my shoulder, then takes the paper from me and scans it. "Oh, shoot," she says when she sees the date. "I'll be on the night shift that night!"

"That's okay," I say, even though it kind of isn't. If my mom has to work, that means I'm going to have to take my dad. Which is fine. I like hanging out with my dad. It's just that sometimes he can be so intense about all the business stuff, and I'm going to be nervous enough waiting to find out who won. I wish I could take Tom. Tom's a very calming influence.

"You'll have to make sure to take lots of pictures," my mom says. After a few minutes of chatting about how exciting the whole thing is, she finally leaves the room.

"So how was your photo shoot?" Jake asks, taking a cookie.

"Um, it was fine," I lie. "The pictures should be out in the next issue."

"Did you have to wear weird clothes?"

"Weird clothes?"

"Yeah, aren't models always wearing weird clothes, like big dresses or whatever?" Jake shoves two cookies at once into his mouth. "I saw it on *America's Next Top Model.*" I give him a look. "My mom was watching it!"

"I don't care if you were watching it," I say. "You shouldn't be embarrassed about something like that; that show is for everyone."

"I wasn't watching it!"

"Okay," I say. "And no, we got to wear whatever we wanted." I decide to change the subject in case he's thinking about bringing up the fact that I'm completely

unphotogenic. Plus we have to get back to the task at hand.

"Anyway," I say. "So what were we talking about before my mom came in here?" Of course I already know the answer.

"How you're going to some lame sleepover and can't play Guitar Hero?"

"No, after that," I say.

He frowns. "I don't remember."

"I think we were talking about how you never get secrets passed to you," I say.

"Right." He pulls the top off an Oreo and licks out the cream. "And then you gave me the secret that was passed to me, and I took it, and then your mom came in."

"Right, and you read it and—"

"Oh, crap," Jake says, looking at the clock on my nightstand. "I gotta go. Leo's coming over. Anyway, let me know if you change your mind about your sleepover and want to play Guitar Hero with us."

He grabs two Oreos for the road, and then he's gone.

Sigh. I thought for sure he was going to tell me what the note said! Why didn't he tell me what the note said? Even if it said she liked him, why wouldn't he want me to know?

Unless maybe . . . he likes her back?

Six

AN HOUR LATER, I'M STANDING ON
Emma's porch with Daphne, and she's really not too
happy. Daphne, I mean. About going to the sleepover.
She was halfway complaining the whole ride over
here. The only reason she didn't ramp it up into full-
on complaining was because Tom was in the car, and
it was impossible to get too cranky, because for some
weird reason, he was playing a CD of Christmas carols.
In September. Which was pretty funny.

But now that we're at Emma's, I have a feeling Daphne
might switch over into full-on complaining. Which I can
kind of understand, since Emma wasn't exactly all that
nice to Daphne. But we should be determined to have a
fun night. I mean, everyone deserves a second chance.
Plus I might need Emma's social status to save my

secret-passing business. Not to mention she might like Jake. It's time to keep my enemies close and my friends closer or whatever.

"This is her *house*?" Daphne asks as I ring the doorbell.

"Yeah," I say. "So what?" I'm being nonchalant, because Emma's house is BIG. Like, really big. Like, it has all these gigantic columns, and there's a statue of a lion on the front porch. A lion! Like, with a big steel mane and everything!

"It's just so *big*," Daphne says.

"Daphne, she's nice," I say.

"Are you forgetting that she wants to marry Jake?" Daphne's looking distastefully at the lion statue. Then she reaches out and pats it on the head. "I wonder what this guy's name is," she says.

"I've decided to name him Alphonso." I, too, give the lion a pat on the head. "Good boy," I say. "And she doesn't want to marry Jake." Why is no one coming to the door? I don't even hear any footsteps. Shouldn't there be a but-ler or something?

"Please, please, please try to have fun," I tell Daphne. "It'll be fine, I swear; she invited you, she wants to be friends."

"She asked if you could trust me!" Daphne says.

"I know, but she didn't mean it, she was just nervous, because she didn't want anything getting out about Olivia's business. She was looking out for me."

"I guess," Daphne sighs. "But I'm serious, Samantha, if she—"

The door gets flung open then. "Hiiii!" Emma yells. She grabs one of my arms and one of Daphne's arms and pulls us into the house. "Come on, we're karaoking!"

"Um, okay," I say. She's leading us through a maze of hallways now, and her house is so big I don't even know where the heck we're going. "Um, where are we going?" I ask.

"To the karaoke room!"

Right. I should have known. I look over at Daphne, who just rolls her eyes.

Be nice, I mouth.

Fine, she mouths back.

The karaoke room turns out to be part of Emma's basement. Like, a big part of it. And when I say "basement," I mean it in a very loose sense of the word. The whole entire downstairs is refinished, with a big-screen TV in one corner, all these floppy chairs and couches, a big floor-to-ceiling bookshelf crammed with books, and a bar in the corner.

Charlie is standing by the TV, in front of a big karaoke

machine, messing around with some buttons. On the screen, a Jordin Sparks video is playing.

"Hello," Charlie says coolly. "What do you two want to sing?" She says it like we might just be so lame that we won't know any of the songs they have, and might need a special CD, like *Karaoke for Losers* or something.

"They have to get into their karaoke outfits first," Emma says. "What did you two bring?" Then she opens Daphne's bag where she dropped it on the floor and starts rummaging through it. She just starts going through Daphne's stuff! Like it's hers or something. Which is a total invasion of privacy, I mean, what if Daphne has something embarrassing in there?

"Why'd you bring these?" she asks, holding up a pair of Daphne's socks. They're pink with green polka dots.

"Um, because I like them," Daphne says. She looks at me, and for a second, I think she might go crazy. Like, have a temper tantrum or something. Daphne doesn't have many tantrums, but when she does, they're not pretty.

"Those socks," Charlie says, "are green." She wrinkles up her nose like she hates green, which doesn't make any sense since she's wearing a green sparkly shirt. Maybe she just doesn't like green socks?

"It's okay," Emma says to Daphne. She gives her a big

smile. "You can borrow something of mine."

"I don't want—" Daphne starts to say, but Emma cuts her off.

"You would look ah-mazing in my black leggings. You have such long legs, you are soooo lucky." She steps back and looks Daphne up and down. "Seriously, you're tall enough to be a model."

Daphne's face softens a little.

"Here's what I brought!" I yell like a crazy person. I want Emma to compliment me, too! I'm not as tall as Daphne, but I do have a pretty kick-butt karaoke outfit. I pull the stuff Taylor let me borrow out of my bag—the silver dress and black tights and ballet flats.

"Oooh, cute," Emma says. "You can change in the bathroom over there." She walks over to the wardrobe standing in the corner and flings open the doors. "Now, this," she announces, "is the karaoke cupboard, and you can pick anything you want out of here to wear." She pulls out a hat. "How do you feel about fedoras?"

"I'm not sure," Daphne says warily.

I take my dress and silver shoes into the bathroom. I wonder why Emma made us bring our own karaoke outfits when she has a whole karaoke cupboard. I start to change, but I'm having a hard time getting the dress on because it's a little big for me and also because I can't tell which is the back and which is the front. Either it's almost backless, or the front is realllly low cut. Hmm. I really should have tried this on.

Someone pounds on the door. "Hello!" It's Charlie. "What are you doing in there? We have to do our makeup!"

"Just a second!" I yell back. I decide to go with backless, so I pull the dress on, then shove my feet into the tights.

I pull open the door.

"Do you want makeup or not?" Charlie asks. It seems vaguely threatening, like she's in charge of the makeup, and if I don't give her the right answer, I won't get any.

"Um, yeah," I say. "I guess." I'm still a little confused about this whole karaoke game.

"Good," Charlie says. "Get back in there."

I walk back into the bathroom, and Charlie pulls out a ginormous bin of makeup from underneath the sink.

"So," I say. "What's the deal, you know, ah, with the karaoke thing?"

"What do you mean?" she asks, frowning. She's rummaging around in the big bin, pulling out tubes of lipstick and cases of eye shadow. Some of them she lines up on the counter neatly, and others she makes a disgusted face at and then drops into the trash can. She's not very environmentally conscious, this girl. First the yogurts and now the makeup. Which is so not biodegradable.

"I mean, so we just do karaoke?"

"Nooo, we get dressed up," she says. "And then we karaoke. And we pretend we're rock stars and sometimes Emma films it with her dad's flip cam."

"Oh. Okay." Charlie pulls out a big compact full of what looks like bronzer. Then she opens it and smears it all over my face. "I don't think I need much bronzer," I say. "I'm actually still pretty tan from the summer, and also I don't—"

"If we record anything, the camera and the lights are going to wash you out."

I decide it might be best not to argue. And honestly, who am I to tell her what's going to look good? I have little to no makeup experience, and the one time I tried to do something beauty-related to myself, I ended up at the salon getting my eyebrows ripped off me in a terrible wax-related incident.

So I stay quiet and watch Charlie as she bites her lip in concentration and does my makeup. She has a smattering of freckles across her nose, which makes her look even prettier than she already is. She works for a while, and then her mouth sort of dips down at the ends, and she steps back a little bit and looks at me. "What's wrong with your eyebrows?" she asks.

"Oh, I have to use makeup to fill them in," I say.

"Because you plucked them all off? Don't you have a good waxer?"

"I do now," I say proudly. "Her name's Jemima and she's amazing. But yes, I plucked them all off."

She sighs, but keeps going. When she's done, it feels like I have about five pounds of makeup on my face. And when Charlie finally lets me look in the mirror, I don't know how I feel about my new, um, look.

"You look very edgy," Charlie says, pleased. "It's like Lady Gaga or something."

My eyes are smeared with purple eye shadow, my lips are lined in a plum lipstick, and I am very, very, very tan. Seriously. I look like Taylor that time she went for a spray tan and the lady working there went a little over-board and then my mom freaked out because Taylor was supposed to have been saving the money she used on her spray tan gone wrong for a new winter coat.

Charlie starts yelling about how I need some fake eyelashes and a hair straightener. "Fake eyelashes!" she yells out the bathroom door to Emma. "Do you have 'em or what?" She's rummaging around in the drawers in the bathroom, where there's apparently every single beauty product or tool you could possibly want, except fake eyelashes.

Emma doesn't answer. I hope nothing bad is going on out there. A few minutes ago I heard her saying to Daphne, "Honestly, with your skin tone, this lime green skirt is PERFECT," and then I sort of tuned out, not really wanting to think about what kind of activity was about to take place in which a lime green skirt was the couture of choice.

"FAKE EYELASHES!" Charlie screams. She pokes her head out of the bathroom door. "Oh," she says. "She's on the phone."

From the other room comes the sound of Emma giggling softly.

"That's okay," I say, sensing an opportunity. "I don't think I really NEED the eyelashes."

"You totally do," Charlie says. "Without them you just look . . . normal."

She says "normal" like it's a bad thing. Also, I most definitely do *not* look normal. Not even close. I look kind of like a clown. But maybe she's right about the eyelashes. Maybe I need to take some chances. Will chances get Jake to notice me? Does he think I'm completely normal since he's known me for so long? Do I need to shake things up? I might be in a rut and not even know it.

From the other room, I hear Emma say in this totally

flirty voice, "You could just *tell* me what it's going to say. Since I'm going to find out anyway."

"Who's she talking to?" I ask Charlie.

Emma laughs loudly from the other room. Charlie rolls her eyes. "She's obviously talking to some guy. You can tell by the way she's being all giggly."

Some guy? Yes! If Emma's talking to some guy, maybe she'll get together with him! And maybe she'll forget all about Jake! In fact, maybe she likes one of Jake's friends, like Leo Wheeler. Maybe she just sent Jake that note to be like, "Hey, I like your friend, can you ask him what he thinks about me?" because she was too embarrassed to tell him in person. And that's why she said she usually doesn't play games!

I stick my head out of the bathroom so I can try and figure out who she's talking to. If Emma *does* like Leo, maybe Emma, Jake, and I will double date! Or at least all hang out in a group. Of course, Daphne would feel left out, but I'm sure we could find a boy to bring for her.

But when I finally focus on what Emma's saying, Daphne feeling left out is the least of my worries. That's because Emma is lounging on her big poufy couch, her legs draped over the side, her long red hair in a perfect halo around her on the cushions. And then she giggles again and says, "No, Jake, I told you . . . if you're going to send a note back, then just tell me what it's going to say!"

Her words are like a horrible dagger to my heart. And the worst part? Emma's on *my* phone.

"I saw his name on the caller ID and so I answered it," she says, like it's no big deal. Which it wouldn't be, normally. Normally, as in, if I didn't like Jake.

"Oh, it's no big deal," I say. "I was just wondering why he was calling me."

"He didn't say," she says, handing me back my phone. "He had to go, he was going to spend the night at Leo something-or-other's." Just like that, my double-date fantasies disappear into the night.

Daphne, who had apparently been sent up to Emma's room to fetch some sort of gold beaded shirt that Emma thought would be perfect on her during the whole Emma-Answering-My-Phone Incident, is looking nervously back and forth between us. Charlie is still in the bathroom, where she finally located the fake eyelashes. Since there was only one pair, she is gluing them onto herself.

Emma squeals, then grabs me and dances me around the room. "He said he got my note and that he was going to write me back and give it to you on Monday." She looks at me. "Isn't that amazing?"

"Well, I guess it's—"

"I mean, it's so romantic. Passing notes back and forth." Her eyes narrow. "Plus there's something so old-fashioned about actually writing a note to someone, instead of sending a text or an email. It's like . . . retro. Olivia totally sucks; you're way better."

Daphne clears her throat, and when I turn to look at her, I notice for the first time that she's wearing a lime green miniskirt over black leggings. Which is so not Daphne.

"You look fab," Emma says. She pulls a flip cam off the bar in the corner. "And now," she says. "It's time to karaoke. Charlie!" she screams. "Get out here so we can sing."

We karaoke for most of the night. Fast songs, slow songs, duets. We change outfits a million times. We film ourselves, and then spend some of the night uploading the footage and editing it into music videos using Emma's dad's computer software.

"If they come out good enough, we'll put them on our Facebook pages," Emma declares. "Or enter them into one of those online karaoke contests."

We order pizza at 1 a.m. from the twenty-four-hour pizza place down the street, then sit around Emma's huge glass kitchen table, eating slices and planning our revenge against Olivia.

"What you have to do," Emma declares, "is beat her at her own game."

"What do you mean?" I ask. I take another delicious, globby bite of pizza off my plate, and wash it down with some lemonade. I can't believe I can eat at a time like this—meaning when Emma has basically told us she's in love with Jake, and when Jake might be in love with her.

The thing is, I'm kind of having a lot of fun. Yeah, Emma and Charlie are a little over the top with their karaoking and their fashion (they seem to favor fedoras, feathers, and anything fake—eyelashes, fur, etc.), but they're also really fun and nice. And besides the whole "I want to date Jake" thing that Emma has going on, I think we could really be friends.

"I mean that you have to start an online secret business as well," Emma says. "Expand into the twenty-first century!"

"But you said earlier that something about passing notes the old-fashioned way was romantic." Honestly, all these conflicting messages are not good for my mental state.

"Well, it is," Emma says, "but maybe you could do

both, you know, like have an online part, and a regular part that you just do out of your locker. Just like Olivia."

"But then wouldn't she just be copying Olivia?" Daphne asks from her seat next to me.

"I still think you should read the secrets," Charlie says. She's eating a salad with gluten-free, fat-free, sugar-free dressing because the sauce on the pizza aggravates her acid reflux.

"I told you, I can't," I say. I take another bite of my pizza. "It would totally ruin my reputation, and my business would be over."

"Whatever," Charlie says. "I'm sure people, like, *expect* you to read the secrets." She rolls her eyes.

"No, they don't!" I say, shocked. "They would never pass things through me if they thought I was reading everything. And if they *did* think I was, they'd totally use Olivia over me."

"It doesn't matter," Emma says. "Because Olivia's not going to keep this up."

"What do you mean?" Daphne asks. "She's not going to keep what up?"

I take another sip of my lemonade.

"I mean that she's a quitter," Emma says. "Like last year when she tried to start up this collection to help the needy? She ended up keeping, like, half the money for herself so she could buy a new iPod and a sweater for her dog." She spears a piece of salad on her fork, then dips it in the pile of dressing that's on the plate next to her.

"She did not!" Daphne exclaims.

"Well, it wasn't, like, *proven* or anything," Charlie says. "But it was a little weird that everyone was giving money, and like, she had none for the needy. But she somehow had a new video iPod and this totally expensive sweater for Bitsy."

"She sounds like a brat," Daphne declares.

"She is," Emma says. "But I'm totally right about her being a quitter. So really, there's nothing to worry about. You just have to wait her out until she gets sick of the dumb secret-passing." A worried look comes over her face. "I mean, not that secret-passing is dumb, I just meant that her trying to steal your idea was dumb. Of course I don't think that what you're doing is dumb; I think it's awesome." She smiles.

"It's okay," I say. And then she's off and running, telling some story about her mom and this new car the family wants to buy. I guess that's it for our strategy session.

Later, when Emma and Charlie are asleep, Daphne and I whisper. The karaoke room has two big couches that pull out into queen-sized beds. Charlie and Emma are sleeping on one, and Daphne and I are on the other. The best part is that the couches are far enough away from each other so that even if Charlie and Emma *were* awake, Daph and I could whisper without anyone hearing us.

"So that wasn't that bad, was it?" I ask.

"Which part?" she says. "The part where they made me wear a lime green miniskirt, or the part where they filmed it and are now going to put it on their YouTube channel?"

"Not their YouTube channel," I say, giggling. "Their Facebook pages."

"Oh, right," she says. "They only put it on YouTube if the lighting is right and they think it can go viral." We both giggle, covering our mouths to muffle the sound.

"Thanks for coming," I whisper. "You're a good friend." I grab my cell off the table next to us and check the time. It's 3:09 a.m. I scroll through until I get to my received calls. "What do you think Jake wanted?" I ask Daph.

"I don't know," she says. She sounds a little strange. I turn to look at her, but it's so dark that all I can really see are shadows.

"Do you think I should call him back tomorrow?"

"Yes," Daphne says.

"Are you sure?" I press.

"Look," she says. She props herself up on one elbow,

her blond hair falling over her elbow and onto the bed. "If this were last summer, and Jake called you, would you call him back?"

"Of course," I say. "But this isn't last year. This is *this* year, and everything is totally different."

Daphne sighs.

We both lie there quietly for a few minutes. From the other bed, the soft sounds of Charlie and Emma breathing fill the room.

"Hey, Daph?" I whisper again. "You asleep?"

"No."

"Do you think he likes me?"

"I don't know."

"Do you think I should tell him that I like him?"

Daphne hesitates, then finally she sighs and says, "I don't know."

Silence.

"Daph?"

"Yeah?"

"Thanks for coming with me."

"You're welcome." Daphne squeezes my hand under the blanket, and then I flip over onto my stomach, bury my face into my pillow, and try to fall asleep.

Seven

ON MONDAY MORNING BEFORE SCHOOL
Eric Niles is waiting for me at my locker.

"Didja see this, did you see this, SAMANTHA?" He's really screaming. Eric Niles is very excitable. I think it's from eating all that paste in the third grade. It probably messed with his brain chemistry or something.

"Yes, Eric," I say. He's holding one of Olivia's flyers in his hand, moving it back and forth, back and forth. It's shaking so much that the papers tacked up on the wall behind us announcing all the new school clubs are fluttering around like crazy. That's how much wind he's generating. I had no idea he was so strong. His arms are like toothpicks.

"*First* of all, Samantha," Eric says, "you look very pretty today. I really like your dress."

"Thank you," I say, pleased even though it's just Eric. He *is* a boy, after all. My dress is really simple, light blue with puffy sleeves and a cotton skirt that flares out a tiny bit at the bottom. I never really wear dresses to school, but Emma let me borrow it when I was leaving her house over the weekend, and I thought it would be fun to wear it today.

"*Second* of all," Eric presses, "did you know, Samantha, that Olivia's business is booming, and she is hoping to expand it even more and is maybe even looking for a business partner?" He dangles the flyer in front of my face.

"Let me see that," I say, grabbing it.

"We have only been open for two days!" the flyer says. "But we have received such a huge surge in business, that we apologize if it is taking us a little long to get to your secrets, LOL! Keep them coming. Also I might be looking for a business partner, so if you want to, please email Olivia@tellmeasecretmillboro.com."

"What the heck," I say, "is she even talking about? *A business partner?*"

"I don't know," Eric says. He looks nervous, and he shifts his weight back and forth between his black dress shoes. "I just found it taped up by the art room, and I thought maybe you should know about it, but now on second thought . . ." He chews his lip. "I didn't want to upset you, Samantha. I don't ever want to *upset* you."

I look up from the paper. Crap. Eric looks like he might start crying. "No, no, Eric," I say quickly. "This isn't your fault."

"*What* isn't his fault?" Daphne asks, walking down the hall and joining us. I hand her the flyer wordlessly.

"Hmm," she says. "Who says 'LOL' in a job posting? And a business partner? She can't be serious."

"Well, internet-speak is becoming more mainstream, with a record number of people of all ages using internet messaging services and texts to communicate," Eric chimes in helpfully.

"Thanks, Eric," I say. "But I don't think internet-speak is really appropriate for a business flyer, do you?"

"No, Samantha, absolutely not," he says. He looks even more nervous now.

"What are you wearing?" Daphne asks me.

"Emma's dress." I do a little twirl, the skirt flying out around me. I wait for Daphne to compliment it, but she says nothing. "You don't like it? You said it was cute when Emma pulled it out of her closet on Saturday morning."

"No, I like it," Daphne says. "I just didn't know you were going to be wearing it to school."

"Why wouldn't I wear it to school?"

"Because you never wear dresses to school." Daphne's looking down at the floor now, and she has a really weird look on her face. Like maybe she wants to tell me something, but can't. I know because I've seen that look on her face before. It was last year, when I let her borrow Taylor's gray hoodie without asking Taylor and then Daphne's cat threw up on it and there was no way to get the stain out.

"True, but there's no time like the present to start switching things up!" I say. Daphne just scowls. "Okay," I say, crossing my arms. "What's going on?"

"Nothing," Daphne says. She looks down at the ground. "I just didn't think you'd be wearing Emma's dress, that's all."

"Wait a second," I say. "Is this about me being friends with Emma? Because she wants to be friends with you, too, Daph."

"No," Daphne says. "It's not about that."

I want to say something else, but I don't know how much I should push, and besides, Eric is standing right there. I don't like getting into friendship confrontations in front of other people. Especially in front of Eric, since he gets real nervous if he thinks I'm upset. And he's worked up enough already.

"What's going on?" Jake asks, walking up to our

group. "Why is Daphne scowling and looking like that time when her cat threw up on your sister's sweatshirt?"

"She can't figure out why Samantha is wearing a dress to school," Eric says. Which kind of proves how clueless he is, since that's not really what we were talking about at all. And then Eric takes a step closer to me, probably because Jake's here now.

I sigh. Eric and Jake don't exactly, um, get along. The really bizarre thing is, it has nothing to do with the fact that I like Jake, because Eric doesn't know I like Jake. *I* didn't even know I liked Jake until a few months ago. Eric doesn't like Jake because he thinks *Jake* likes *me*. Eric thinks *everybody* likes me. It's kind of flattering.

"Why are you wearing a dress?" Jake asks.

"I just felt like it." Suddenly, I'm annoyed. I mean, really. Who cares if I wore a stupid dress to school? People wear dresses to school all the time! Everyone's acting like it's some kind of huge global event. Don't they know there are people dying in Darfur? I might have to get Candace from the photo shoot to email them some information so they can increase their social awareness.

"Yeah," Eric says. He moves another step closer to me. "She felt like it!"

"Anyway," I say, waving the flyer in my hand. "Forget about the stupid dress. We have bigger problems here."

It's not on the level of Darfur, but it's still pretty important. At least to me.

Jake takes the flyer and reads it.

"Yikes," he says.

"I know," I say. "Emma said Olivia's a quitter, but it doesn't seem like it."

Daphne rolls her eyes and mutters something that sounds like "What does Emma know?" but I'm kind of not paying that much attention because I'm too busy watching Jake's face for any reaction to Emma's name. But he doesn't move a facial muscle; it's like his face is made of stone or something. I decide to push it a little bit. "That's what *Emma* said when I was at her sleepover this weekend. You know, when you *called* me?"

"Yeah," he says, "I wanted to see if you had Julia Tibbot's number. We were going to invite her brother over to skateboard, since you didn't want to come."

"It seems as if Samantha had *plans*," Eric says. He moves even closer to me. "So she couldn't come to your little skateboarding party." He says "skateboarding party" like Jake had been planning to take me to a gang fight or something.

Daphne says, "I can't believe you're wearing a dress."

"Get off the dress!" I almost scream. "We have THINGS TO DEAL WITH!"

"Look," Jake says. "You have to stop freaking out about this whole Olivia thing. Just take it for what it is— competition. Nothing to get all worked up about yet. How many secrets are in your locker right now?"

I look. "Three," I say.

"Is that normal for this time of day?"

"Yes," I say. "Three's about right."

"So there you go," he says. "Keep an eye on what this Olivia girl is doing, and if it seems like your business starts falling off, then you might have to come up with a plan. Until then, it's just a minor annoyance." Hmm. I guess he might be right. I *could* be freaking myself out over nothing. I *can* be extremely dramatic like that.

Jake readjusts his book bag on his shoulder and smiles at me. "It's going to be fine, Samantha."

Eric glares at him. The bell rings then, and Daphne says, "Gotta get to homeroom" and then heads down the hall without even really saying goodbye. What is up with her? She and I are going to have a serious talk at lunch.

The boys head to class, and I turn around and start gathering the books I need for the morning, along with the three secrets that were left in my locker. There's a tap on my shoulder as I'm sliding the last secret, a note for a girl named Miri Jones, into my bag.

It's Jake. "I forgot to tell you one thing," he says. "I like your dress. I think you look really pretty in it."

Oh. My. God. I can feel myself blushing, all the way from the top of my forehead down to my toes. He did not just say that! I take a deep breath and try to think of something witty to say. I lean against my locker and wrap a strand of my hair around my finger, the way I've seen Taylor do when she wants a guy to notice her.

"You came all the way back to tell me that?" I say, and give him my most winning smile.

"Uh, no," Jake says. He reaches into his pocket and pulls out a folded-up piece of paper and holds it out to me. "I came to give you this."

I look down at the paper, hoping it's some kind of note for me in which he confesses his love and all the things he's too shy to say to my face. But it's not. It's a secret that he wants passed. It's held together with a paper clip, and there's a dollar on top, and the name on the front says EMMA.

"Why would he send her a secret *back*?" I ask Daphne. It's lunch, and Daphne and I are working in the computer lab, since Daphne wanted to work on the story she's doing for the school paper. I think it's way too early in the year to be working on the school paper (I mean, no news has even really happened yet), but their first meeting is on Wednesday, and, according to Daphne, it's super hard for seventh graders to get any kind of responsibility. Apparently there's some eighth-grade editor in chief who's on a big power trip and has told everyone that the seventh graders will get no assignments unless they're really, really good. Everyone who wants to be on the paper was asked to bring a sample story, and so Daphne really needs to make a good impression.

"Because *she* sent *him* one?" Daphne tries. "He was probably just being polite and writing her back." She's still clicking away on the computer next to me, her fingers flying over the keys.

"Yes, but that doesn't make any sense; it's not a note-passing service, you send one secret and then you're done. If he likes her back, then why doesn't he just tell her?" I bite my lip and press the mouse on the computer I'm using. I'm playing Snood, this game where you line up little creatures into patterns and then zap them away. It's kind of a lame game, but it's one of the only ones they have on the school computers. Anything cool is either blocked or not able to be downloaded.

"I don't know, Samantha," Daphne says. "Maybe because they think it's cute or romantic or something."

"Yes, but if that's true, then why did he say that about my dress?"

Daphne sighs. "You do know that's the fiftieth time you've asked me that, right?"

"Yes," I say, realizing Daphne's probably getting pretty sick of my little anecdotes and freak-outs about Jake and Olivia. I decide I need to work on being a better friend. "What's your story about?" I ask.

"Global warming," Daphne says.

"Wow," I say. "Ambitious."

"I'm writing about the global epidemic, but my article is going to focus on the things we can do here, as a school, and how kids can get into being green."

"That sounds cool." Daphne gives me a look. "What's that look for?" I ask. "I'm totally into being green!" I am, too. Well. Sort of. I do recycle. Or at least, I try to remember to recycle. And yeah, maybe *sometimes* I accidentally leave my air conditioner up too high while I'm sleeping. But only on really hot nights. And I always turn it off when I leave the house or even the upstairs. Most of the time.

"Listen," Daphne says, "I'm sorry about the way I acted about your dress this morning." She starts playing with the corner of her notebook sitting next to her on the computer desk.

"It's okay." I say. "But what's going on? You've been acting really weird ever since we spent the night at Emma's."

"I don't know." She's still fiddling with her notebook.

"Daph," I say. "Whatever it is, you can tell me. Seriously, it's—"

I'm cut off by a voice. A very loud voice that's talking *so* loud that it carries over the whole bank of computers to where we're sitting. And that voice is saying, "I know, it's so lame, like, you leave a *dollar* in her locker? How 1990 can you get?"

"You weren't even born in 1990," another voice says. "So how would you know?" And then the two voices combined start to giggle.

"Ohmigod," I whisper to Daphne. "They are *so* talking about me!" Who else could it be? I'm the only one who gets dollars in my locker!

Daphne holds her finger to her lips, so that we can hear the voices better.

"Anyway, Olivia," the second voice is saying. "How much money have you made so far?"

"Twenty dollars just today," the first voice (obviously Olivia) says.

Twenty dollars! What a liar! There's no way she made twenty dollars just this morning. I mean, on my best day ever, which was Valentine's Day of last year, I only made about ten or fifteen dollars. Of course, I was in a much smaller school then, but still. Twenty dollars in one day?

Less than a week after she started, at the beginning of the school year, when no crushes or scandals have even had time to start? Impossible!

"Twenty dollars?" her friend says. "That is so awesome!"

"I know," Olivia says. "But honestly, that Samantha girl has really done me a favor. Since she's running such an old-fashioned operation, people are super psyched to work with me. A lot of the people don't like the idea that there's an actual paper out there with their secret on it. They love that everything's digital, which is why I'm raking in the money." I hear the vibration of what sounds like maybe her cell phone. "Oh, there's another one right now," Olivia says. "Make it twenty-one dollars. And this one is totally prepaid."

My mouth's open so wide my jaw feels like it might be on the floor. I look over at Daphne. Her eyes are the size of saucers, and her eyebrows are all the way up almost to the top of her forehead.

"Don't you feel bad?" Olivia's friend says. "For ruining that poor girl's business?"

"Not really," Olivia says. "In fact, I want to end her. That's life in the big city." A bunch of giggling follows this pronouncement, which totally makes no sense. *That's life in the big city?* Do they know we don't even live in the big city? I guess it's just a figure of speech, but still. And *end* me? Gosh. That sounds very . . . dramatic. And kind of scary, like something you'd see in a gangster movie.

We hear the sounds of chairs scraping, and then the clack of heels against the floor, which get fainter until they're gone. When I think it's safe, I pop up out of my chair to see if I can get a glimpse of her, but it's too late. She's gone.

"Oh my God," Daphne says. "She's totally after you."

"I know," I say. "What am I going to do?"

"I don't know yet," Daphne says. "But this means war."

"War?" I whisper. I don't know if I'm ready for war. War sounds serious. War sounds like something you do when you're really down and out. "I don't know if I'm ready for war," I say.

But that afternoon, there's not one secret in my locker.

eight

"THERE WASN'T EVEN ONE SECRET!" I rant. I'm in my kitchen, after school, going through the pantry looking for snacks. I'm pulling out Cheetos (no), chips (no), granola bars (omg, def no), until finally I locate a jar of Nutella on a shelf in the back. I pull it out, then grab a loaf of bread and a spoon.

"Well," Tom says. If he's startled by my outburst, he doesn't say anything. He's sitting at the kitchen table, reading the paper and drinking a cup of green tea. Tom's super into antioxidants. "Maybe it was just a fluke. A *coincidence*, if you will."

"Tom," I say. "She said she was going to *end* me, and then there were no secrets in my locker. That kind of sounds like the beginning of the end to me, doesn't it to you?"

"Maybe, maybe not," Tom says.

"Do you want a sandwich?" I ask, remembering my manners despite the total and complete professional and personal crises that have befallen me lately. Who knew middle school was going to be so complicated? And it's only the second week! At this rate, things definitely do not bode well for high school.

"What kind are you having?

"Nutella." Tom looks at me skeptically. "What?" I say. "It's totally healthy, it's on wheat bread! Plus it has hazelnuts in it; those are way high in antioxidants."

"Okay," Tom agrees, still not looking so sure. I fix the sandwiches, slap them onto plates, and plop down in the seat next to Tom.

"The worst part," I say, "is that when this whole thing happened, it totally distracted me from the fact that I was talking to Daphne about why she was acting so weird about my dress. And I got all caught up in it, and I didn't get to work anything out with her."

"Why don't you call her?" Tom asks.

"I texted her." I sigh. "But she's at the newspaper meeting, and I'm not sure what time it's going to be over." We both chew our sandwiches thoughtfully.

"It's been a bad day for me, too," Tom says sadly. "Aren't you wondering why I'm home from work early?"

"Not really," I say. "Sometimes you come home from work early."

"Yes, well, today the reason I came home early was because we had this huge luncheon, where the new VP of sales was announced."

"Oh, right," I say. "Weren't you up for that?" I remember Tom staying up late one night last week, trying to get his résumé in tip-top shape. Those were his words, not mine. I don't say things like "tip-top shape."

"Yes." Tom takes another bite of his sandwich. "But I didn't get the job. So now I'm home early, because they let everyone leave after lunch. Unless, of course, you were Doug Dugan, who got named the new VP of sales. Then you got to stay and get 'shown your new office,' which really means you see your office and then get taken drinking all afternoon with the partners." Then Tom looks startled, like maybe he just remembered I'm only thirteen. "Out drinking Cokes," he says. "Of course."

"Wow," I say, deciding this calls for a lie. "That doesn't sound like a very fun job description. Hanging out with the bosses? No, thank you."

"It's actually the best job ever," Tom says sadly. "And you get a raise."

"It's okay," I say, reaching out to pat his hand. "We don't need the money." We don't. My mom is the nursing supervisor at her hospital, and she makes more than enough money to support the whole family.

This is definitely the wrong thing to say, though, because Tom gets an even sadder look on his face. Tom *never* gets even sadder looks on his face! It's probably kind of weird for him for my mom to make more money than he does. *I* don't think it's a big deal, but I guess Tom does. And it probably doesn't help that my dad is this super successful businessman who makes way, way more than my mom and Tom. Maybe even more than both of them combined.

Hmm. I really should not have said that. But then I think of something that could totally cheer Tom up!

"Hey, Tom," I say, "do you want to go to the *You Girl* banquet with me?" When I talked to my dad this weekend, he told me he would be out of town on a business trip that night. Which I was kind of slightly relieved about. So I was planning on asking Tom anyway, but this just seems like the perfect time to do it.

Tom's whole face lights up. "I'd love to!" he says.

"See?" I say, hopping down off my chair and heading to the counter to make myself another sandwich. "I'll bet if you were a dumb VP you'd have to work that night, and you wouldn't even be able to go."

"The vice president does have to put in a lot of extra

hours," Tom says. He takes a big bite of his sandwich.

"You see? And they probably never get to make any of their own decisions; they always have to ask the dumb president if they can do things!"

"Yeah!" Tom says. He really is like a kid sometimes. "This sandwich is really good." He looks at it thoughtfully. "Who would've thought? Chocolate and hazelnut on a sandwich."

"Tom," I say seriously. "Who *wouldn't* have thought?"

The phone rings then, and I grab the cordless to answer it, even though it won't be for me. Everyone I know would call my cell. But to my surprise, the lady on the other end actually *is* looking for me.

"Samantha Carmichael, please," she says, sounding all professional. "Speaking," I say back, just as professionally.

"Hello, Samantha," she says. "My name is Barb Davies, and I'm one of the senior editors at *You Girl*."

Oh. My. God. Oh no, oh no, oh no. She must be calling because my pictures turned out completely terrible! I'm probably going to have to go down to New York and redo them. Or even worse, maybe they're going to drop me from the issue altogether! They'll cite space issues or something, but really everyone will know that it's not the space at all. It's the fact that I'm unphotogenic. Stuff like that totally happens. Everything is completely image-based now, I'm sure even for America's number one tween magazine. I wonder how many people tried to Photoshop my eyebrows before they just gave up. This is the most embarrassing thing that has ever happened to me

"Nice to speak with you," I say politely. Then I decide to cut her off at the pass. "If you're calling about the photo shoot, I'd like to apologize right now. I'd had no sleep that day and my train ride into the city was just a nightmare." That's something I heard my mom say once. That her train ride into the city was just a nightmare. It's a very grown-up type of thing to say.

"What?" Barb asks. "Oh, no, this isn't about the photo shoot, those pictures came out fine."

Phew. "Well, thank you," I say. "I mean, I'm not really that photogenic, but obviously the makeup helped and—"

"Yes, well," Barb says, cutting me off. I guess she doesn't have that much time, since she's probably really busy running America's number one tween magazine. "The reason I'm calling is because we've picked a few of our finalists to do some short profiles on. We plan on including them with our announcement of the Young Entrepreneur of the Year in our next issue, and we've chosen you as one of those girls. Of all the finalists this year we felt yours was one of the more contemporary, fun businesses and we think it would translate nicely to the page."

"Oh my God!" I say. "That is amazing!" How cool is that? Take *that*, dumb Olivia and your dumb internet secret-passing business. Barb just called my business "fun" and "contemporary"! Contemporary! That totally means current, hip, in the now. Actually, now that I think about it, I should have been playing this *You Girl* finalist thing up as much as I could. Olivia hasn't been in *You Girl*, now, has she? No. Ha!

"Yes, we're all very excited about this year's finalists," Barb says.

"So, yes," I say. "I say yes to the profile."

"That's wonderful," Barb says. "Now, we're going to need to send someone to your place of business to shadow you."

"What do you mean?" I ask.

"I mean," she says patiently, "that we will send a representative, meaning me, to your place of *business* to watch how you work, how you run your office, that kind of thing."

"Oh, well, I don't have a place of business," I say. "So that idea, unfortunately, won't work for me at this time." That's another phrase I've heard my mom use.

That something won't work for her at this time. It usually gets her out of anything. But Barb's not having it.

"It doesn't have to be an *office*, necessarily," she says. "Most of our *You Girl* entrepreneurs don't have offices, since they're tweens. I was using that word more symbolically."

"Yes, well," I say, "I work from school—from my locker, if you will."

"Oh, wonderful!" Barb says. "We would love to be able to send me and a camera crew down to your school to follow you around!"

"Follow me around?" And a *camera crew*? It was bad enough that I had to have my picture taken at a studio. I don't know if I can handle a camera crew. That sounds very stressful. Not to mention the biggest problem, which is that my business has started, ah, floundering. I don't think that's going to translate as well to the page as Barb hopes.

"Yes." The sound of keystrokes comes through the phone. "I'll call your principal to set it up."

"You will?" My mouth is suddenly very dry.

"Yes, usually the schools are thrilled to have us!"

Okay, then. "Um, when will you be coming?" I cross my fingers that it's far, far away so that I have time to prepare.

"Let's shoot for sometime next week." Great. So I have less than a week to somehow get my business back on track, so that when Barb and her camera crew show up, I won't look like a total jerk. Not to mention hope that my eyebrows are still camera ready.

"That sounds perfect," I lie.

"Thanks so much, Samantha!" Barb says. She sounds extremely happy and perky.

I replace the receiver and walk gloomily back to the table. "They're going to spend a day shadowing me," I say. "They're coming to my school."

Tom chews his Nutella sandwich thoughtfully. "Well," he says. "You just need to get back on track." He reaches over and squeezes my shoulder. "It will be fine."

"Right," I say. But I'm not sure either one of us really believes it.

Later that night, I surf around on my computer, looking up facts for my social studies research paper on the ancient Mayans. And maybe since I'm already online and everything, I just *happen* to check out Olivia's website. She's calling her business Olivia's Secrets. I know this because it's splashed across the header of her site. Also, that name is extremely generic. Of course, I don't even *have* a name for my business. Which is even more generic. It's like, how would people even know how to find me? I'm just "Samantha Carmichael, the girl who passes secrets."

To make matters even worse, my dad called earlier and we got into this whole discussion about the importance of branding and I came to the conclusion that my business is definitely a total branding fail. I mean, I don't even have a logo! I didn't have the heart to tell my dad that branding myself is the least of my worries right now. How could I? He would be so disappointed if he knew my business was falling apart. Instead I told him about how they're sending a camera crew to my school. He loved that.

I'm contemplating starting an account on Olivia's site so I can check out the competition, when my cell rings.

Jake!

"Hey," he says, "I just wanted to check on you since you seemed pretty upset this morning."

"Yeah, I was," I say. "Well, I still kind of am." I squint at Olivia's website. "And now things have gotten worse, since (a) *You Girl* is sending a camera crew to school to shadow me, and (b) I'm looking at Olivia's website, and it's pretty amazing."

"They're sending a camera crew?" Jake sounds interested.

"Yeah," I say. "To see what I'm doing, and the head of the whole magazine is coming, this very scandalous woman named Barb."

"Why is she scandalous?"

"Not scandalous, I guess, just scary." I sigh and abandon the computer to move over to my bed, then plop down on my green and yellow comforter. I stare up at the ceiling and decide to feel sorry for myself.

"Don't worry," Jake says. "You're going to be fine."

"I don't know," I say. "You should see this website, seriously. It has this completely interactive interface."

"Interactive interface?"

"Yeah."

"Do you even know what that means?"

"Yes," I say. "It means that the interface is interactive. Duh." Seriously, boys can be so dumb.

"Okay," Jake says. "Look, we'll figure it out." My heart speeds up a little bit when he says "we'll." It's very . . . couple-y. Like we're in this together.

"Will we?" I ask, mostly because I just want to try out how it feels to call Jake and I a "we." It sounds good. Perfect, even.

"Yes," he says. "Look, do you want to meet at The Common tomorrow morning before school? We could get danishes and I'll bring my laptop and you can show me this lame website you think is so great."

I think about it. First, I am not a morning person. Second, The Common is actually just a fancy name for a special cafeteria at our school. It's the caf they used to use before they built a new one, and now they open it before and after school so that kids can hang out and study. Third, I am going to have to get Tom to agree to drive me there. Fourth, I don't care, because JAKE IS INVITING ME TO THE COMMON! Is this a date? Probably not. But still. He wants to hang out with me. Alone. Not with Daphne or Emma or anyone else!

"Sounds good," I say. Me and Jake alone. Not that I've never been alone with him before, but obviously it's different now. Completely different. His new voice is just one part of the whole "now this is different" puzzle. Why, oh, why did I wear Emma's dress today? I should have worn it tomorrow, so I could be super cute for my date with Jake. I mean, my not-date with Jake. My sort-of-date with Jake? Whatever, the point is, I should have worn it tomorrow.

"Great," he says. "Meet me at seven forty-five or so?"

"Okay," I say.

"Oh, one more thing," Jake says. "Did you ever give Emma my note?"

Sigh.

nine

"HE MUST LIKE HER, DAPH," I SAY THE next morning, turning my head completely toward the windows of the cafeteria so that no one can tell I'm on my cell. "Otherwise why was he freaking out about me giving her the note?"

The thing is, I *did* give Emma the note. I gave it to her after lunch. And I didn't read it. Of course I *thought* about reading it, I *obsessed* about reading it, but somehow, I was able to control myself. It was very hard. Especially when she started opening it as she walked away down the hall, and I probably could have looked over her shoulder and tried to sneak a peek. But I didn't.

What I don't get is, Jake knows I would never read a secret, or hide a secret, or accidentally on purpose lose a secret. I don't think he even knows I've thought about doing those things. So there was really no reason for him to ask me if I gave that note to Emma. Unless he was really, really anxious and wanted to know if Emma got it. Which means he probably likes her, too. Right? I mean, why else would he be freaking out about it? This is what I'm debating with Daphne on the phone while I wait for Jake at a table inside The Common.

"Samantha," Daphne says, "so what? He'll be over it in two weeks. That's about how long seventh-grade crushes last."

"That is so not what I want to hear." Two weeks? How am I supposed to go through two *weeks* with Jake liking Emma and Emma liking Jake and the two of them passing notes back and forth like two little crazy note-passers with nothing better to do than to make my life miserable? Two weeks is a lifetime! Two weeks is, like, fourteen whole days. Three hundred and thirty-six hours. Twenty thousand, one hundred and sixty minutes. That is forever. And wow, I am really good at math.

"I know it's not what you want to hear." Daphne sounds grumpy. Probably because I woke her up at six a.m. asking her what I should wear to go meet Jake. I tried to call and text her a bunch of times last night, but she never answered.

I finally settled on my favorite jeans, my new comfy

sweater boots, and a red-and-blue-striped sweater. It's a very cute outfit. It was actually a blessing that I wore Emma's dress yesterday, because otherwise I would have been obsessing over whether or not I should wear it. And now that I think about it, that dress really is way too dressy for school.

"Listen," I say now to Daphne. "We need to talk later. About why you're mad at me."

"I'm not mad at you," she says.

"But in the computer lab yesterday—"

"Look, I'm not mad," she says. "Now I have to go; my bus is going to be here soon. I'll see you at school."

She hangs up. I sigh and look out the window. Jake's mom's van is pulling up in the circle out in front. I pull a magazine out of my bag and pretend to be reading it.

"Hey," Jake says when he gets to my table.

"Oh, hey." I try to sound surprised, and peer at him like maybe I even forgot he was coming. "I didn't see you there."

He looks at me funny and then slides into his chair. "Yeah, well, here I am," he says. "Do you want a drink?"

"Sure," I say. "A lemonade would be fab." I reach into my bag and pull out my wallet (it's from last year and has a rainbow on it with clouds—sooo embarrassing— but I haven't gotten around to buying a new one, and besides, how can I afford a new one now when my business is going kaput?) and pull out two dollars. I try to hand it to Jake, but he waves me off. "I got it." He heaves his computer bag up onto the table. "Can you boot it up while I go wait in line?"

"Sure," I say. Ohmigod! Jake is buying me a lemonade! Hello! That is like one step away from a date. Isn't it? I mean, that's what happens on dates. Guys buy the girls something. Like a lemonade, for example. Also, Jake has left me in charge of his computer! Jakes loves his computer. It's not something he would let just anyone touch.

I pull it out of the bag slowly, careful not to drop it. It's a MacBook Air that Jake named Wilfred. (I know, how cute, right?) Jake saved up all his Hanukkah money and all his birthday money, and then worked, like, three hundred hours at his dad's landscaping business to make up the difference. It's sleek and shiny and he loves it.

The computer is almost booted up (Jake's background is a picture of his dog, Sylvester, even cuter) when the door to The Common opens, and Emma and Charlie come waltzing in. Well. It's more like strutting. Seriously, they look like they're on a runway at Fashion Week or something. And what are they *doing* here? Not that I mind seeing them exactly, it's just . . . when you're on a maybe-date with the guy you like, you don't want the girl he's been passing secrets with to show up. That just, you know, doesn't really work.

I bury my head in my magazine and decide to try and ignore them.

"Samantha!" Emma yells, waving like a maniac. Sigh.

"Oh, hi," I say. I peer up at them like I really didn't even see them come in. This look might be starting to become a thing with me.

"What are you doing here?"

"Oh, uh, same thing you are," I say, trying to be deliberately vague.

"What is Jake's computer doing here?" Charlie demands. "And his bag?"

"How do you know what Jake's computer looks like?" I ask before I can stop myself.

"We see him here all the time," Emma says. She sits down. Across from me. In Jake's seat. "Anyway, I have another note for him." She slides it across the table to me, with a dollar clipped to the top. Oh, for the love of . . . I look down at it and try not to let my face betray what I'm feeling. Which is *OHMIGOD, WHYARETHESETWOPASSINGSOMANYNOTES?* Also, maybe they should just *LEAVEMEALONEANDGOTRY-OUTOLIVIA'SSECRETS.*

"Thanks," I say. My voice sounds strangled.

"I gotta go," she says, looking over her shoulder nervously. "I don't want to be here when you give it to him." Then she and Charlie move over to the other side of The Common, where they plop down at a table, pull out their math books, and start giggling.

I run my finger over the note. What the *heck* are they passing notes about? The curiosity is killing me! Honesty, I might just be about to go crazy. One little look wouldn't hurt, would it? Just one look. At one note. I know I said I would never do that, but aren't these kind of, like, extreme and extenuating circumstances? Mental torture, even?

I glance over to make sure Emma and Charlie aren't looking, and then I slide my finger under the note, ready to break the tape. I can tape it back up later, when I get to homeroom. Or first period. Or home. Or somewhere. I don't know, I'm not thinking straight! I'm like a woman possessed! I reach under the tape and it's about to break ohmigod it's going to break and I'll finally find out what—

"Here you go!" Jake sets a bottle of lemonade down next to me and I scream.

A couple of people turn to look. "Geez," Jake says. "What's your problem?"

"Sorry," I say. "I was, um, so engrossed in this article that you scared me, haha." I grab the bottle of lemonade and take a sip. Luckily, Emma and Charlie are so far away that they didn't seem to notice me shrieking.

"Is that for me?" Jake asks. I follow his gaze to the note that's sitting on top of my magazine. I pull the dollar off of it slowly, slip it into my rainbow wallet, and hand the note to Jake. "Yes," I say. "It is."

"Is it from Emma?" He looks excited.

"Yes," I say again. "It is."

"Thanks." He puts it into his bag without reading it, then turns back to his computer. "So should we look at this site or what?"

"Sure," I say. I can't believe he actually wants to do work! How can he not notice that I'm freaking out, that I'm completely and totally upset by the fact that he is passing notes with Emma? And why is he not reading it? If he was so excited to get it, then why doesn't he just READ THE DARN THING?

"Hmm," Jake says, tapping at the keys and looking at the screen. "Okay, so it seems like she has a pretty easy system set up here. Very user-friendly."

"Great," I say. I take another sip of lemonade. "Easy and fun and just what everyone wants."

"You could do this," Jake says. "You could get something like this set up—it would only take maybe, like, five hundred dollars."

I laugh. "And where, may I ask, am I going to get five hundred dollars?" I apparently now can barely even get *one* dollar, much less five hundred.

"I wish I knew more about coding," Jake says. "But I don't. Otherwise I would totally build you something." Jake's more into hacking than coding. One time last year he was even able to hack into our superintendent's email account. He could have set up a fake snow day and everything, but he didn't. He *says* it was because he was only doing it for the challenge, but I think it's really because he knew he could probably get arrested or kicked out of school or something.

"That's really sweet of you," I say.

"We could always set you up a website with some kind of template," Jake says.

"Oh, yeah," I say. "Like some crappy template website is going to compete with *that*." I gesture to the screen, where the OLIVIA'S SECRETS header is now blinking and flashing. I lean back in my chair. God, what a disaster.

Then, out of the corner of my eye, I see Emma and Charlie wave at Jake from the other side of the caf. "So you see Emma here a lot?" I ask, as Jake waves back at them.

Jake shifts in his chair uncomfortably. "Um, not

really," he says. "I come here a lot in the morning to go over my math notes." Jake has a hard time in math, and I know his mom told him last year that if he didn't keep his math grade up, he'd have to stop skateboarding.

"Oh," I say. For some reason things get awkward for a second, and Jake and I just sit there not saying anything, and then suddenly, the door to The Common goes flying open, and Eric Niles rushes in, his backpack bouncing roughly against his back. He's wearing one of those hats with the floppy ear flaps, and they're flapping all over. His face is red.

"Samantha Carmichael!" he yells. "Samantha Car-michael, where are you?" He looks all around, and even though I'm sitting right there, his eyes slide past me. I guess because he's in such a panic.

"I'm right here," I hiss. Everyone is looking. So extremely embarrassing.

"Oh, Samantha, thank God I found you!" Eric pulls a chair up to our table and plops himself down. Great. So far, on what I thought was a maybe-date, I've been asked to pass a note to Jake from Emma, and Eric Niles has shown up and is now sitting at the table with me and Jake, like a complete date-crasher. One hundred percent *not* the way I imagined this morning going.

"How did you know I was here?" I ask, trying to keep

my voice light. I don't want to be mean to Eric, since he *is* nice and usually pretty harmless. Of course, he is also an inconsiderate date-crasher, so I don't know how long my self-control will last.

"Your stepfather told me," he says. He sets his book bag down in the middle of our table. Then he starts pulling a bunch of papers, books, and folders out of it, piling them all up.

"You talked to Tom?" I ask. This thought is worrisome. Tom's so nice to everyone. He might have invited Eric over to the house to hang out or something. Tom loves inviting people over. One time in fourth grade he invited my whole class over for a pottery painting party. It didn't go so well. The paint turned out to be nonwashable, and we'll just leave it at that.

"Yes," Eric says. "I called your house because you weren't answering your cell."

"What are you doing?" Jake asks. He looks down at all the stuff Eric is dumping on our table. The pile now includes half of a roast beef sandwich in a baggie, and some green plastic army men.

"Aha!" Eric says. "Here it is!" He pulls out a crumpled piece of paper and smooths it out. It's covered in pencil writing.

"What is that?" Jake asks.

"It's a record of what I'm about to tell you." Eric looks at us seriously over his wire-rimmed glasses. "Now, first, I have to preface this with an apology."

"Okay," I say. I feel nervous. Usually if Eric is starting out with an apology, whatever he's about to tell you definitely can't be good.

"I . . . I . . ." He looks at me. "Well, I guess I'll just say it." He takes a deep breath. "Samantha, I used OLIVIA'S SECRETS TO PASS A SECRET!"

"You *what*?" I shriek. Not because I'm really that mad, but because I can't believe *Eric* would do something like that. Eric is supposed to be in love with me. He's not supposed to be going around using Olivia's website to pass secrets! That's like cheating on me. God, everything in my world has gone totally and completely crazy and out of whack.

"I know," he says. And then he gets out of his chair and throws himself at my feet. "I'm sorry! I will make it up to you, Samantha, I will, I swear it!"

"Eric," I say. His mouth is coming very close to my shoes, and I'm afraid he might try to kiss my feet or something. Hello, embarrassing. "It's okay, get up."

"Yeah," Jake says, not looking at all amused by this crazy display. "Get up."

"What should I do?" Eric says. He gets up and plops

himself down in a chair. "Do you want me to carry your books to every class for you? Should I make you dinner? Do you want me to do your homework every day for the rest of the school year?"

"Dude," Jake says, "you need to chill."

"Yeah," I say. "Chill. It's okay, Eric, I'm not mad."

"You're not? But I betrayed you!" He's almost wailing now.

"It's okay," I say.

"Well," he says. "If you say so." He chews on his bottom lip. Then he takes a deep breath. "I have to tell you something else."

"There's more?" I ask warily.

"There's more?" Jake asks. He looks like he might want to strangle Eric.

"Yes," Eric says. He gives Jake a dirty look, then sits up in his chair and adjusts his glasses. "And I think, Samantha, that you will want to hear this." He gives Jake a pointed look.

"Okay," I say uncertainly.

"It's kind of confidential," Eric says. He looks at Jake again.

"You want me to *leave*?" Jake asks.

"It's okay," I say quickly. "Jake can stay, he's cool."

"Yeah," Jake says. He gives Eric a look. "I'm cool."

"All right," Eric says. "I guess." He doesn't sound so convinced. "So anyway, the reason that I was using Olivia's Secrets in the first place was because I wanted to find out what your plans were for Halloween."

"You wanted to find out what whose plans were?" Jake asks.

"Samantha's."

"Then why didn't you just ask her?"

Eric looks at Jake like he's crazy and has no idea about how to get girls. "Because it was going to be a surprise, which is why I didn't pass the secret through Samantha. She knows my handwriting, and I figured she would know something was up."

"Why didn't you just have someone else write Samantha's name on it?" Jake asks.

Eric sighs, pulls his glasses off, and looks up at the ceiling, like he's dealing with a child. "Because the secret wasn't for Samantha, it was for Daphne. I wanted to ask Daphne if Samantha had plans for Halloween. But if I passed a note to Daphne through Samantha, then of course Samantha would ask Daphne who the note was from. I couldn't take the chance that Daphne would crack and ruin the surprise."

"Why didn't you just ask Daphne to her face?" Jake asks.

Eric blinks. "I don't know," he says. Oh, for the love of . . .

"*Anyway*," I say. "Can we please focus here?"

"Right," Eric says. He slides his glasses back on and sits up very straight. "So I passed Daphne a note asking what you were doing for Halloween, and how you would react to us possibly going trick-or-treating as Romeo and Juliet. You know, if I asked you beforehand." Eric's whole face gets red, and his ears turn red too.

"You wanted to go trick-or-treating with Samantha as Romeo and Juliet?" Jake asks.

"Yes." Eric clears his throat. "It's a play. By Shakespeare."

"Yeah, I know what it is," Jake says, his voice tight.

"Aww, that's sweet, Eric," I say. It is, too. Not that I would really want to go trick-or-treating as Romeo and Juliet with Eric. I don't think I'm dressing up this year. I might be a little too old for that whole thing.

"Yes, well, I'm getting to the best part," Eric says. He rubs his hands together gleefully. "So this morning, I'm walking along, minding my own business—" Jake snorts at this part, I guess because he can't really imagine Eric minding his own business. Which kind of makes sense when you think about it, since Eric is usually very much completely up in people's business. "*Anyway*," Eric says.

RULES FOR SECRET KEEPING

"I was minding my own business, just walking along to The Common, when all of a sudden, I walked by Brooke Highsmith and Tucker Levangie. And do you know what they said as I passed by?" Eric lowers his voice and looks around, getting ready to lay the punch line on us.

"No," I say. "What did they say?" For the love of God, spit it out.

Eric looks down at the paper, where he's apparently constructed a written record of the whole incident. "They said, 'Oh, Romeo, Romeo, wherefore art thou, Romeo?' and then they laughed." Eric sits back in his seat and looks smug.

"Um, okay," I say, not really getting it.

"That's pretty funny." Jake chuckles and takes a sip of his hot chocolate.

"Don't you *see*?" Eric says, shooting Jake a dirty look. He moves his chair closer to mine. "Those two knew my secret! Olivia told them! She is READING THE SECRETS!"

My mouth drops open and I sit up straight. "Are you sure?"

"Yes!" he says.

"You didn't tell anyone else about the Romeo and Juliet idea?" I ask him.

"No!" He shakes his head from side to side vehemently.

"I didn't! I sent the secret as soon as I came up with the idea."

Jake laughs again. I shoot him a dirty look of my own, because honestly, he's being a little bit of a jerk. Eric is perfectly nice, and besides, he is giving me important information here. Important, possibly life-changing information.

"Eric," I say. "I might love you just a little bit right now." Eric beams.

"It doesn't matter," Jake says, shaking his head. "You need proof."

"We *have* proof," I say. "Eric heard two girls talking about a confidential secret that he passed. A secret that he didn't tell anyone else."

"That's not really proof," Jake points out. "It's just one person's word against someone else's."

"It *is* proof!" I insist. Even though I know in my heart that he's right. It would be Eric's word against Olivia's. And who's going to believe Eric? Everyone knows he's been in love with me for, like, ever.

"He's right," Eric says stiffly. "But I'll help you to bring them down any way I can."

"Actually," Jake says. "Samantha and I were just talking about that. Do you know anything about computers?"

"Not really," Eric admits. For all his geekiness, Eric

is more into earth science, math, and video games. He doesn't get too much into the techy, hacker side of geekdom.

"Well, I think this website is highly unsecured," Jake declares.

"You do?" Eric asks.

"Yeah," I say, frowning. "You do?" And why is this the first I've heard of this?

"Yes." Jake looks at me seriously, and then he looks at Eric triumphantly. "And I'm going to help you hack it, Samantha. If we can hack into it, we can prove her whole online business is completely vulnerable."

"This," Eric says, propping his glasses up onto his nose, "is war."

"You two," I say, "are the best!" Eric keeps beaming. But Jake just looks annoyed.

ten

"IT'S WAR," I TELL DAPHNE WHEN I SEE her at her locker before homeroom. Of course, this might be overstating it just a little bit. I mean, of course it's not war *exactly*. Also, I don't know much about waging war on someone. I might have to ask Taylor and/or Emma for tips. Those two probably know lots about it.

"What's war?" Daphne asks.

"The whole secret-passing thing." I fill her in on what happened at The Common.

"Jake really thinks he can hack into the site?" She sounds doubtful, and she keeps putting her books into her locker really slowly, not looking at me.

"I don't know," I say. "Of course, I have no idea how easy it will be or if he knows what he's doing. But he's going to try! And that means we're going to be spending a lot of time together." I raise my right eyebrow up and down suggestively, trying to make her laugh. But she doesn't. Which means something is definitely wrong. Daphne usually loves it when I wiggle my right eyebrow up and down. It's a very hard thing to do, to wiggle only one eyebrow. Plus now that my eyebrows are half-painted on, it should be, like, doubly funny.

"What's wrong?" I ask. "Seriously, Daph, let's talk. Whatever it is, we can talk about it, I swear. I want to, I—"

"I told you," she says. "It's nothing." But she slams her locker door shut more forcefully than I would deem necessary. So I'm pretty sure she has some pent-up anger boiling around inside. "I have to get to the newspaper office to drop off my story. And then I'm going down to the gym to talk to Coach Krasinksi about soccer."

"I didn't know you were joining soccer," I say.

"Yeah, well, there's a lot of things you don't know lately." And she takes off down the hall before I can say anything else.

Geez. The high I had for a little while when I heard that Olivia might be reading people's secrets is totally gone. How can I be happy when Daphne's mad at me? And not just, like, normal mad at me, but really, really mad at me. I mean, she's not even telling me about the things she's doing, like trying out for soccer! How horrible is that? I *always* know what Daphne's doing, and she always knows what I'm doing.

And then, as if out of nowhere, comes the perfect solution to my Daphne-related problems. A flyer on the wall, announcing our school's Fall Festival. It's, like, this completely big deal, with a hayride and a corn maze, and maybe even some other, lamer stuff that teachers think will be fun but really isn't, like bobbing for apples. And everyone is supposed to bring a date, but I can ask Daphne to go with me! It's not like we're going to have dates. We can eat candy apples and ride the hayride and go through the big corn maze and it'll be totally fun.

Yay! I'm so excited that when the bell rings for lunch, I wait outside the cafeteria for Daphne, hoping I can cut her off before she goes in.

"Hey," I say.

"Hi," she says.

"You wanna sit outside today?" I ask. I hold up my bag. "I have a Nutella sandwich and half of it has your name on it." Hopefully she likes Nutella as much as Tom does.

Daphne hesitates. "What about Emma and Charlie?" she asks. "Won't they be upset if you're away from them for two days straight?"

"No," I say. "I'll tell them I had to make up a test or

something." I don't really care if Emma and Charlie get mad. This is about me and Daphne. We need to reconnect and work on our friendship. Hmm. That sounds like a totally fab article for *You Girl*: "You and Your BFF: How You Can Work on Reconnecting." I should bring that up to Barb when she comes to shadow me next week. I wonder if they're looking for writers. I could totally be a tween correspondent or something.

Daphne and I head outside to one of the big stone benches in the courtyard. We set up our lunches between us and then straddle the bench, facing each other. It's a gorgeous day, still warm enough to be outside without a jacket, but the air smells of fall, and the trees are shedding leaves in all different colors.

"So listen," I say, unable to contain my excitement. "Do you want to go to the Fall Festival together?"

"Together?" Daphne frowns.

"Well, yeah," I say. I rip off a bite of my Nutella sandwich (made by Tom—he is much better with the Nutella than with the tuna fish, thank goodness. Also, I think Tom might have started to develop a little bit of a Nutella problem. The other night I came downstairs and found him eating it right from the jar with a spoon), and pop it in my mouth. "I mean, I know we're supposed to ask boys or something, but let's face it, there's no way I'm ever going to work up the courage to ask Jake. Were you planning on asking someone?"

"Nooo," she says slowly. "I just didn't think you'd want to go with me. I thought you'd want to go with Emma."

"No," I say. "I'm not going with Emma." And then I remember the note Emma gave me this morning. "She, uh, sent Jake another note this morning."

"*Another* one?" Daphne screeches. She looks really angry for some reason—her face gets all red and her eyes get all crinkly around the edges. "Seriously, Samantha, this is getting ridiculous. If you're not going to ask either one of them what they're passing notes about, then we're going to have to start reading them."

"Ohmigod, no!" I say, "I can't. And besides, you're one to talk about how people should be telling secrets. Why didn't you tell me Eric asked you if I would dress up as Romeo and Juliet with him for Halloween?"

"Oh, God." Daphne rolls her eyes, then takes a bite out of the other half of my sandwich. "I *knew* he wouldn't be able to keep that to himself! I found an 'anonymous' printout in my locker. It said: 'Dear Daphne, Do you think that Samantha would be interested in being Juliet for Halloween if a secret admirer was her Romeo? Also the only reason I am using this service is so that Samantha won't find out. I am a loyal customer to her, please know that.' 'Loyal' was underlined, like, five times and in italics." She giggles.

We spend the rest of the period talking about how she's nervous about her newspaper story (she doesn't know if it's any good or not), about how we really need to go shopping together soon (Daphne has no cute sweaters and I really need a new corduroy skirt), and about how Taylor's boyfriend is starting to grow this very weird-looking mustache (it's getting long and skinny and sometimes I see him stroking it when he thinks no one's looking).

It's just like old times, and by the end of the period, I decide that Daphne got so upset about my dress that day because she was feeling left out since I started hanging out with Emma and Charlie. I have to make more of an effort with her, and things will go back to normal super quick, I just know it.

A few minutes before the bell is going to ring, my cell starts vibrating in my bag.

"It's *You Girl*," I say, rolling my eyes. "Probably that crazy woman from the other day."

"You should take it," Daphne says. She glances over her shoulder toward the school. "Miss Morris is on lunch duty, and you know she spends the whole period trying to make sure the eighth-grade boys don't give each other wedgies. She won't even notice you're on your phone. Besides, I have to run to the newspaper office before the period's over."

She gathers up the garbage from her lunch, drops it into the trash by the door, and heads into the building.

"Samantha Carmichael speaking," I say into the phone. "And how may I help you, please?" I'm hoping Barb will think I answer the phone like that all the time, like maybe this is my business line, on which I'm always doing busy and important business things. Hopefully this will distract her from finding out that my business has basically fallen apart in, like, two days, and that the only business I'm really getting is from the boy I'm in love with and the girl who is trying to steal him away.

"Yes, Samantha, this is Barb." She doesn't sound too impressed with my greeting.

"Hi, Barb," I say. I glance over at Miss Morris. She's trying to stop Brandon Jacobs from giving Justin Dumont a wedgie. You can tell Brandon's gearing up to do it because he's all lurking around the side of the building, getting real close to Justin and mumbling something that sounds like, "Wedgie wedgie wedgie, who needs a wedgie?" Ugh. *Boys.* "I can't talk that long," I tell Barb, "because I'm at school, and my studies are very important."

"Yes, yes," she says. "Of course, I understand. I just wanted to let you know that I had a lovely conversation with your principal this morning, and our crew has been invited to document you next Tuesday."

"That *is* lovely," I say, wondering how I'm going to explain it to her when she finds out there's no business, no notes, and nothing to really document. Miss Morris has averted Brandon's wedgie quest and is glancing around the whole outside lunch area now, so I duck down under the bench and pretend to be looking for something on the ground. "So if that's all . . ."

"Yes," she says, "We are so looking forward to it."

"Me too," I say. "I mean, I am also."

"Goodbye, Samantha."

"Goodbye, Barbara." Oops. She never really referred to herself as Barbara before. Just Barb. But I would assume her name is Barbara right? Isn't everyone who's called Barb really named Barbara? Or can you just be named Barb? I was trying to sound all formal, but I don't think it really worked. It kind of sounded disrespectful. Oh well. I click off the line and the phone rings again in my hand.

My dad. My dad never calls me during the day.

"Hello?" I say. "Dad?"

"Samantha," he says. "Why are you answering your phone at school?"

"Why are you calling me at school if you don't want me to answer?" I mean, really.

"I wanted to leave you a message."

"Well, when you call me at school, I feel like there might be an emergency, and so I answer my phone." I'm still on the ground under the bench, pretending to look for some imaginary object. My hand brushes against an empty candy bar wrapper. Ewww.

"But aren't you not supposed to be answering your cell phone at school?"

Oh, for the love of . . . "Yes, Dad, but I'm at lunch." I'm trying to keep my patience, but it's starting to get seriously frayed.

"Ahh, excellent," he says, obviously assuming that this somehow means we're allowed to talk on our cell phones at lunch, which is so not true. "Anyway, the reason I'm calling is because I have fabulous news."

"You do?" I hope this fabulous news doesn't take too long to relay, since the bell's about to ring.

"Yes," he says. "It turns out that I've locked down the Istanbul deal ahead of schedule, and since I had intended to go to Turkey to have a face-to-face, my trip there has been canceled."

"Good for you," I say, not sure why he's calling me at lunch to tell me all this. I mean, it's great that his trip is canceled, since he hates to fly and the flight to Turkey is like a bazillion hours long. He gets really nervous up in the air, which is kind of funny, since my dad is not the type to get scared of anything. But when he flies he totally has to take all this medicine. He even went to a hypnotist once. But I guess it didn't really help.

"Soo," he says. "That means I'll be able to go to the *You Girl* dinner!"

"Oh." I swallow. "That's great." Of course, I already invited Tom. But I guess I'll just have to tell him he can't go. I hope he wasn't set on it or anything. Out of the corner of my eye, I can see Miss Morris walking over to the side of the courtyard where I'm crouching under the bench.

"Okay, well, see you later," I say to my dad.

"Samantha—" he starts.

"Gotta go." I hang up and quickly straighten up. "Oh, there was that note I was looking for!" I say real loud to no one. And then I walk quickly into school.

eleven

AFTER SCHOOL, I'M WALKING TO MY
bus when someone tugs on my ponytail. Jake.

"Do you wanna come over later tonight?" he asks.
"We could brainstorm about the website."

"Sure," I say. Hanging out with Jake twice in one day!
Yay! I guess he just can't get enough of me. I mean, he's,
like, obviously desperate to hang out with me.

"You don't *have* to," he says, "if you don't want to.
I just thought we could try to see if we can hack into
Olivia's site."

"Okay," I say. So much for desperate. But that actually does sound pretty fun. And kind of intriguingly
dangerous. Hacking into things. Am I going to become
a hacker? Maybe Jake could teach me how to hack into
all kinds of different places. Maybe it will be my new

business. Although I'm not sure *You Girl* would look too fondly on me if I started becoming a hacker. But I'll bet it's very lucrative.

"Cool," he says, then disappears into the throng of kids on their way to their buses. I stand there for a second, watching his blue backpack bounce through the crowd until I can't see him anymore.

"Hey, Samantha!" Emma says from behind me. "Was that Jake?"

"Uh, yeah," I say. And then before she can ask, I say, "I, uh, gave him your note this morning."

"Thanks." She wraps a strand of her long red hair around her finger. "So where were you at lunch?"

"Oh," I say. "I ate outside." I decide not to mention the reason why. No sense making Emma think that Daphne doesn't like her. Those two have enough problems.

"Well, next time it would be, like, nice to let me know." She rolls her eyes. "I saved you a seat!" She says it like saving a seat was this big imposition, even though there's, like, five empty tables in our lunch period. "Anyway, do you want to come to Charlie's aunt's consignment shop after school? We're going to find stuff to wear to the Fall Festival."

"I can't," I say. "I have plans tonight." I decide to leave out the part about those plans being with Jake. Is that weird? That I'm leaving that out? I mean, Jake and I are *friends*, I have the right to hang out with him. Plus if Emma and Jake are passing secrets, I certainly have the right to keep a secret of my own. Don't I? I mean, it's like quid pro quo or whatever they call it. An eye for an eye. A tooth for a tooth. A secret visit for a secret note.

"Oh, come on," Emma says. "My mom can pick you up at four, and you'll be home by six. The store is right downtown."

I think about it. It *would* be fun. And Jake did say "later," which probably means after dinner. Plus I don't think I should start planning everything around when Jake wants to hang out. I mean, we're not even boyfriend and girlfriend.

"Okay," I say.

"Cool." She grins. "See you at four."

When I get off the bus, Tom's outside working on his car, this old beat-up Buick that he's named Sagamore. Sagamore is constantly breaking down, but Tom refuses to get a new car and/or bring Sagamore in for service. He likes to fix Sagamore himself, and he says newer cars are a waste of money because once you drive them off the lot they lose all their value. I try to tell him that with all the money he spends buying parts and stuff at

AutoZone, it would be worth it, but he won't listen.

"Samantha!" he says when he sees me. "I'm glad you're here; can you hold this flashlight for me?"

I take the flashlight and aim the beam down into the hood. I don't know much about cars, but under the hood it doesn't seem like it's doing too well. Everything is very rusted and dirty. It seems like maybe Tom is attempting to loosen some kind of bolt off of something, but it's stuck and won't turn. He's struggling with the wrench, which also doesn't seem like it's in very good shape. Tom has a lot of tools, but I don't know if they're the right ones. Or maybe he just doesn't really know what to do with them.

"Is it okay if I go to Charlie's aunt's consignment shop with Emma?" I ask. "We're going to look for outfits for the Fall Festival."

"Who's driving and what time will you be home?" Tom asks.

"Emma's mom is going to pick me up, and I'll be home by six." I watch as Tom tries to yank the bolt off. He's starting to sweat a little, even though it's cool out.

"That sounds fine." He peers down into Sagamore's hood. "Wow," he says. "This one's a doozy."

I try not to giggle. Everything with Tom is a doozy. "What are you fixing?"

"Well," Tom says. He points to an internet printout that's sitting on the edge of the engine. "I think the serpentine belt might be going. At least, that's what it said on Google Answers, so I'm trying to replace it. The problem is, you have to remove a bunch of things to get to it." He plucks a leaf out from under the hood and drops it on the driveway.

"Sounds complicated," I say.

"It is," he says. "But in the end the victory will be worth it." He pats the car affectionately. "And old Sagamore here will thank me."

"I guess so," I say uncertainly. I mean, Sagamore can't really thank him, because she's a car. Also, Sagamore would probably be just as happy if Tom took her to the mechanic.

"Oh, I almost forgot!" Tom says. "I got a new suit for the *You Girl* dinner."

Uh-oh. "Oh," I say. "You really didn't have to do that. In fact, I needed to talk to you about that. It's—"

"No, I wanted to!" he says. "Usually I hate shopping, you know that, but this time it was fine, since it was for something I'm really looking forward to."

"Right," I say slowly. "But actually, it turns out that—"

"Now, Samantha." Tom straightens up from under the hood and holds his hand up to stop me from saying anything more. "There is no reason to be nervous. I don't care if you win or lose or if you decide you don't want to do this secret-passing business ever again. You are an amazing young woman, and winning or not winning this award is not going to change that." He smiles. "The suit's gray, and it's rather dashing if I do say so myself."

"Great," I say, weakly smiling back. I am a horrible, horrible person. The thing is, I *want* to take Tom. It would be *fun* going with Tom. But I could never, ever in a million years tell my dad that. He would FREAK out. So as much as I hate it, I have to let Tom know that he can't go. But how can I tell him that *now*? Especially when he's having such a hard time with Sagamore. I feel the start of tears burning at my eyes, and I take a deep breath and try to keep them from developing into the kind of tears that spill down your cheeks.

Taylor comes walking up the driveway then, home from cheerleading, her long hair swinging behind her. "What's with you two?" she asks. "Tom, are you fixing the car again? Ewww, Samantha, you have grease all over your hands."

"I'm replacing the serpentine belt," Tom says happily.

"Yeah, well, you're both filthy." Taylor wrinkles up her nose, then drops her books on the ground and comes over for a closer look. But not too close. She would never risk getting dirty.

Not like me, apparently. There's grease all over my fingertips (how did that happen?), and there's a smudge on my jeans. "I'd better go inside and get cleaned up," I say. "Emma's mom is going to be here any minute."

"Where are you going?" Taylor asks.

"We're going to Charlie's aunt's consignment shop to pick out something to wear to the Fall Festival," I say.

"Ooooh, the Fall Festival," Taylor says in a singsong voice. "So do you have a daaaatte yet?"

"No," I say, narrowing my eyes at her. I can't believe she's bringing up dates in front of Tom! How off-the-charts embarrassing. Although he probably subscribes to the same school of thought as my mom, the one that lets me be alone in my room with a boy because she just can't fathom the idea that anything could happen. "I'm not going with a date. I'm going with Daphne."

"Then why are you going with Emma and Charlie to pick out costumes?"

"I'm not," I say. "I mean, we're not getting costumes. We're getting outfits. Or they are. I'm mostly just going for fun, to get ideas. Daphne and I will probably get our outfits together."

"Everyone goes to the Fall Festival in costume,"

Taylor says wisely. She leans over, touches her toes, then bounces up and down and repeats the movement a few times. Taylor gets tight after practice, so she's always doing stretches. Sometimes she does splits just to show off, which is very annoying.

"What do you mean, everyone goes in costume?" I ask. *Costumes?* Like, Halloween costumes? I really hope Eric Niles doesn't get wind of this.

"Costumes," Taylor says. "You know what costumes are, Samantha."

"Yes," I sigh. "I do."

"Ahh, the Fall Festival," Taylor says. She looks off into the distance, and a small smile drifts across her face. "That's where I had my first kiss."

"Yes, well, I'm sure you girls will have plenty of time to have your girl talk as the festival gets closer," Tom says. He wipes his hands off on a dirty rag that doesn't really do anything except smear the grease around his hands. And then he says, "I'm going to go inside and call Dan down at AutoZone to see if he has that part I need. Looking forward to the dinner, Samantha. Remember what I said."

"I will," I say.

"The dinner?" Taylor asks once Tom is in the house. She pops up out of her stretch, then leans back down and picks up her books. "What dinner?"

"Oh, nothing," I say. "I really have to get inside and wash up." I start crossing the lawn as fast as I can, but Taylor's legs are about three times as long as mine, and she catches up to me in no time.

"Is he talking about the *You Girl* dinner?"

"No," I lie. Which is, of course, fruitless, since Taylor isn't stupid.

"Samantha, you know that dad isn't going on his Turkey trip, right? And that he thinks he's going with you?"

"Yeah," I say. "I know, I just . . . I haven't had a chance to tell Tom yet."

"Well, you better," she says. "You better tell him quick, before he goes out and spends tons of money on some suit that he'll never wear again." Yikes.

"I *know*," I say. "I'm going to."

"When?" she presses.

"Soon." Right after I figure out how to save my business and keep Emma from stealing Jake. Not necessarily in that order.

twelve

"THIS IS AWESOME," EMMA SAYS, HOLDING up a turquoise-and-gold flapper dress that has fringe on the bottom and skims her knees.

"Eww, no," Charlie says. "We don't want to look like we're going as twenties girls."

"Why not?" I ask, fingering the fabric. It's soft and delicate, and it feels silky and perfect between my fingers. If I were looking for a costume, it's what I would want.

"Because last year at our school Halloween party, Jennifer Pritchard showed up wearing a flapper dress, and hers was real, and we would constantly be compared to her. Plus it is way too Halloweeny." Charlie makes a face.

"Oh, right," I say, even though I kind of have no idea what she's talking about.

Charlie's aunt's consignment shop isn't exactly what I pictured. I thought it would be all kinds of, you know, *clothes*. Instead, it's a costume shop. And not even the normal kind of costume shop, like with fake blood and witches' hats and stuff like that. Instead, it's more of a . . . I don't know. A dress-up shop, I guess. Like a consignment shop, only with weirder stuff that people might use to make their own costumes. And it's all used, which I guess is where the consignment part comes in. So I guess it's kind of a consignment costume shop?

Anyway, when we got here, I asked Emma why there were no Halloween costumes, and she looked at me like I was nuts. "Samantha," she said. "You don't go to the Fall Festival in a *Halloween* costume, that is soooo fifth grade. You dress up in a *costume* costume." I didn't really get the difference, so I just said, "Oh, right," and rolled my eyes like I just got confused for a second.

"Oooh, that's right," Emma says now. "Jennifer Pritchard. She's so pretty; did you know that her hair is naturally wavy like that? And it's completely real, she doesn't have extensions or anything." She looks at me and waits for me to be impressed.

"Wow," I say. I don't even know who Jennifer Pritchard is. Like, at all.

"She *is* pretty," Charlie chimes in. "But I wouldn't want to look like her."

"So who do you think is pretty that you would want to look like?" Emma asks.

They start chattering on about who they think is pretty versus who they think is pretty that they'd actually want to look like. I don't really get the conversation. I mean, if someone is pretty, why wouldn't you want to look like them? Unless, of course, you thought that you were prettier than the pretty person in question. The logic of all this is very hard to keep up with, and it's making my head spin.

"Girls." Charlie's Aunt Camilla comes out of the back room, where she disappeared to find us something "perfect" after Emma's mom dropped us off. "I have the perfect outfits!"

From behind her back she pulls out what looks like three scraps of brown fabric.

Emma and Charlie scream in delight and start jumping up and down.

"Um, what are they?" I ask.

"Cowgirl costumes!" all three of them shriek.

Then Aunt Camilla pulls a cowboy (cowgirl?) hat out from behind her back, which makes Emma and Charlie scream even more.

"Oh my God, Aunt Camilla, you are a genius!" Charlie jumps up and down and Emma hugs me.

I don't really get why they're so excited, but I don't want to seem like I'm completely out of it, so I just smile and kind of go along with it.

"And," Aunt Camilla says, her brown eyes twinkling, "I have three of them!"

"Yay!" Charlie says.

"Yay!" Emma says.

"Yay!" I say. And then I realize what they mean. They want me to wear one of those horrible cowgirl outfits. That, of course, is completely ridiculous since (a) I cannot go as a cowgirl. I would look totally out of place in an outfit like that. And (b) I am supposed to be going to the Fall Festival with Daphne, and so we should be coming up with costumes together.

"Oh, I can't." I take a couple of steps back, away from the offending costumes. "But you two go ahead."

"We have to have three," Charlie says. She narrows her blue eyes at me. "Otherwise it's stupid."

"Completely stupid," Emma agrees. "If we don't have three, we won't be able to do a dance or anything."

"A dance?" I don't like the sound of this.

"A step dance," she says. "Like they do on ranches and in cowboy bars out west." I doubt Emma has ever been on a ranch or in a cowboy bar out west, and I tell her as much, but all she says is, "I've seen them in movies and music videos," and then they're both pushing me into the dressing room and the next thing I know I have the cowgirl outfit on.

"This is a little too small on me," I say, surveying myself in the mirror. The skirt is super short with fringe all along the bottom, and the brown vest is tight and if I lift my arms up, it shows a strip of my stomach. "So I guess that settles that," I yell over the door and start to take off the costume. But before I can, the dressing room door goes flying open and Charlie and Emma are standing there in front of me.

"Geez," I say. "Have you ever heard of knocking?" Or better yet, putting locks on the doors? Aunt Camilla says they don't let the energy of the room flow freely.

"You look ah-mazing," Charlie says. She jumps up and down and claps her hands, her hair bouncing.

"Yes," Emma agrees. "It fits you perfectly."

"It's too short," I say, pulling on the bottom of the skirt.

"We'll wear tights under," Emma says. "It'll be too cold without them anyway."

"The shirt is too short too," I say.

"Duh, you'll have a T-shirt on underneath." Charlie

rolls her eyes like she can't believe how stupid I am.

"Wrap them up," Charlie instructs Aunt Camilla.

"I don't have any money," I say.

Charlie looks at Aunt Camilla. "Aunt Camilla?" she pleads.

"For my favorite niece? On the house, of course. Just make sure to send me some pictures." Charlie hugs her. Emma hugs her. I hesitate. And then, finally, I hug her too.

"You're going as *what*?" Taylor asks later that afternoon. I'm in her room, on her laptop, going through my email address book and emailing all the other *You Girl* finalists and Candace. I know it's a long shot, but I'm hoping against hope that maybe one of them might not be able to go to the banquet, or that maybe one of them knows *someone* who can't make it and can give up their ticket. Then Tom and my dad can both go. Of course, I'll have to somehow convince my dad to be in the same room as Tom. But I'll think about that later.

"Shh!" I say. "Keep your voice down." I get up and shut Taylor's bedroom door. I came in here as soon as I got home, so that I could hang out with her and send my email. I was just sitting here typing away and minding my own business and then Taylor asked me what I was going to the Fall Festival as, and at first I tried to lie and say I didn't know, but Taylor can always tell when I'm lying, ever since I was three and she was five and I tried to tell her that I didn't paint her favorite Barbie's hair green. I don't know *how* she knows, but she does.

Anyway, I had to tell her I was going as a cowgirl and now she's freaking out.

"You're going as some kind of wild cowgirl?"

"Not *wild*," I say. "Who said anything about *wild*?"

I read over what I've written.

Dear You Girl *finalists,*

Hi! How are you? My name is Samantha Carmichael, and I am one of the You Girl *Young Entrepreneur of the Year finalists. I met some of you at the photo shoot. Anyway, I cannot believe that the banquet is in a couple of weeks! We are getting so close to finding out who the winner of the* You Girl *Young Entrepreneur of the Year award is! So very exciting!*

As I'm sure all of you are aware, we are allowed two tickets to the banquet. Unfortunately, I have a stepfather and a father, and I'm sure they would both just love to attend. I was wondering if perhaps you or your family has an extra ticket you would be willing to give to me? I am not saying that it is more important for my family to go than yours, of course, but it would help me out greatly.

It was so amazing meeting some of you at the photo shoot, and I hope we can all keep in touch!

Good luck to all!

Best wishes,

Samantha Carmichael

I tried to sound like I wasn't just getting in touch now because I needed something, even though that's obviously the reason. I feel bad about it, but I would feel even worse if I have to break poor Tom's heart. I read the email through one more time, spell-check it, hope for the best, and hit send.

"Well, it *sounds* wild," Taylor's saying. "Cowgirls are *known* for being wild. They ride bulls and, like, lasso people."

"It's not definite that I'm going as a cowgirl." Which isn't a lie. "And I'm definitely not going to *lasso* people, that's ridiculous. Anyway, I told you—I'm probably going to try to find another outfit with Daphne."

"If you say so," Taylor says, not sounding like she believes it.

"Gotta go," I tell her, hopping off her computer chair and heading for the door. "I'm supposed to be at Jake's. Thanks for letting me use your computer."

"You've been spending a lot of time with Jake lately," she says lightly. I turn around. She's on her bed, painting her toenails a color called Pumpkin Spice.

"No, I haven't," I say. I sound defensive. Very defensive. I try it again. "No, I haven't." Yikes. Still defensive.

"Didn't you just have breakfast with him this morning?"

"Not really," I say. "I mean, yeah, we did meet up, but we weren't having breakfast. I mean, yes, I did have a lemonade, but we were mostly getting together to talk about something else. Something having to do with business stuff." Taylor looks at me skeptically, then caps the nail polish she's using and opens her mouth to say something else. But I don't wait for her to catch me in a lie. I slide my feet into my shoes and hop out the door to go to Jake's house.

"Oh, hi, Samantha!" Mrs. Giacandi says when she opens Jake's front door. "So nice to see you!"

"Hi," I squeak. This is the first time I've been over to Jake's house since he came back from camp. The first time I've stood on his mat since I started liking him. The first time I've rung his doorbell. The first time—

"Are you okay?" Mrs. Giacandi asks. "You look a little . . . ah, pale."

"I'm fine," I say. Oh my God! Jake's mom can tell! She KNOWS THAT I LIKE HIM. Moms are very good about picking up on that stuff. And now maybe she's going to tell him. Maybe they'll sit down to breakfast tomorrow and she'll be all, *"Wow, that Samantha was acting very flustered last night; she really has a crush on you, Jake."* And Jake will be all, *"Yeah, I kind of noticed that, it's weird. I want to be friends with her, but not if she's going to get crazy."* And then Mrs. Giacandi will be all, *"Jake, you know girls at that age are very vulnerable; I don't think you should be friends with her if it's going to mess with her mind."*

"Jake's upstairs," Mrs. Giacandi says, closing the door behind me. On second thought, maybe she doesn't know, if she's willing to let me go up to Jake's room without worrying about us. What is with everyone? Is it so strange to think that Jake and I could like each other as more than friends? Or do people just think it's weird that Jake could like *me* as more than a friend?

I bound up the stairs, which doesn't really help the fact that my heart is racing. Jake's bedroom door is open, and he's at his desk, his back to me, playing a video game on his computer. He has his headphones on.

"Hey," I say. But he doesn't hear me. He's moving his hands and arms all around, trying to kill something on the screen. Or outrun something. It's hard to tell.

Whatever it is, it looks very violent and loud. Also maybe a little bloody. I think it's one of those video games parents are always protesting against.

"Hey!" I say again. Still, he doesn't hear me.

I take a few steps toward him. I wonder if I should, like, touch his shoulder? Or maybe just scream his name really loud. "JAKE!" I yell. He doesn't turn around. Finally, I reach out and touch his shoulder.

He screams and throws his controller up in the air. "Ahhh!"

"Ahh!" I scream back. On the screen, a dragon starts to beat Jake's character into a bloody pulp. Gross.

Jake laughs and pulls his headphones off. "Sorry," he says. "You scared me."

"No, *I'm* sorry," I say. "I was calling your name but I guess you didn't hear me. Since, you know, you had your headphones on." I'm babbling, so I take a deep breath and then grab a chair that's leaning against the wall. I pull it over toward the computer but not, you know, too close. No need to tip him off.

"What are you doing way over there?" Jake asks. "Can you even see the screen?"

"Uh, no," I say. I scoot the chair closer and throw my bag over the back. I hope he won't be able to notice my drawn-on eyebrows when we're this close. Jake, of course, looks fabulous. He's wearing a Tony Hawk T-shirt and a pair of baggy cargo pants.

"Now," he says, pulling up Olivia's website. "If you look at what Olivia has set up, basically her website form gets filtered into a normal email account." He taps around on the screen and shows me. "So if we can somehow prove that her email account is corrupt, then we can break into her emails and prove that the whole system isn't secure."

"But *is* it corrupt?" I ask, trying out the word. Corrupt. It sounds so . . . sinister.

"Well, it's not corrupt per se," he says. "She just doesn't have any security measures in place." He types around some more, opening up a program that asks him for the email password. "So if we can figure out her email password, then we can probably get into her account."

"Try 'IhateSamantha,'" I say.

Jake laughs. I love making him laugh! I reach over and pretend to type "IhateSamantha" into the computer, and at the same time Jake reaches over to type something, and our hands brush against each other and he doesn't pull away right away and neither do I and my face gets all hot and electricity runs all the way from the tips of my fingers down to my toes, making me all tingly.

I yank my hand back, and Jake looks over at me and smiles, and then just keeps typing like nothing happened.

"So, uh, what are you doing now?" I ask. I slide my hands into my lap and will myself to keep them there so that there are no more mishaps.

"Well, I tried all the normal passwords she might use, like 'Olivia' or the name of her dog, or 'ZacEfron.'"

"How did you know the name of her dog?" I ask.

"I found it on her Facebook page."

"Oh, right. And Zac Efron?"

"She has Photoshopped pics of herself with him in her photo gallery."

"Right." I giggle.

"So now I'm just running a simple hacking program that's going to try and find out the password."

"Do you think it will work?"

"I don't know," he says.

I watch as the program runs on the screen, and suddenly, out of nowhere, I feel like I want to cry. It seems so pointless. Trying to bring down Olivia's Secrets, when really all she did was figure out a way to do what I was doing, only better. What am I going to do when Barb comes to my school next week? I have no clue if things will even be back to normal by then. How am I going to figure out a way to mask the fact that I am basically getting no secrets anymore? And to top it all off, what the heck am I going to tell my dad?

"What's wrong?" Jake asks, noticing the look on my face.

"Nothing." I try to make my voice sound bright. "Just tired, probably from getting up so early." I give him a tentative smile.

"Right," he says, rolling his eyes. "Seriously, what's wrong?"

"Nothing!"

"Samantha," he says. "We've been friends since we were eight, you can't tell me nothing's wrong when something definitely is."

"Well," I say, taking a deep breath. "It's just that Barb is coming to school next week to follow me around for *You Girl*. And I haven't really been getting any secrets anymore." An image of Barb standing in front of my locker while I open the door to see nothing there flashes through my brain. "And she's going to think I'm a total loser." My throat is catching on itself, and I'm trying not to start crying.

"You'll be fine," Jake says. "You'll think of something, you'll fix it."

"Maybe I will, " I say. "But not in time for when Barb comes. And then there's the whole mess with the *You Girl* dinner. Do I bring Tom or do I bring my dad? Now that I've realized there's probably, like, no chance I'm going to win, I know I should probably bring Tom. My dad will freak out if I don't bring him, but if I *do* bring him and I don't win, then, then . . . and . . . and . . ." That's when I lose it. I start to cry, the tears sliding down my face.

"Oh," Jake says. "Umm . . ." He shifts in his chair and looks uncomfortable.

"Sorry," I say, wiping my tears with the back of my hand. "I don't know why I'm crying, it's so silly."

"It's not silly," Jake says. He reaches over to the box of tissues on the top of his desk and hands me one. I blow my nose. Great. Totally what I want to be doing in front of the guy that I like. Getting all sniffly and gross.

"I mean, I know it's just a dumb secret-passing website. It's not a matter of national security or anything. It's not even something that makes a difference in people's lives. Did I tell you there was a girl at the photo shoot who was making bracelets to save the children in Darfur?"

"Well, that's awesome that she's doing that," Jake says. "But that doesn't mean that what you're doing is any less special. You put in just as much work as she did."

"Not really." I sniff. "I haven't even tried to research the way the digital revolution is sweeping the nation. Or work on my branding. Or come up with a name for my business. And now I'm paying the price."

"The digital revolution?" Jake looks confused. "Samantha, Olivia didn't research the digital revolution, she just happens to have a dad who knows about computers and set her up with a website so that she wouldn't have to do any real work."

"Maybe." I sniff.

"And you watch, once we prove that she's telling people's secrets, or once we can get into her website, she'll lose interest in this whole project and move on."

"You think?"

"I know." And then something crazy and wonderful and horrible and exciting and terrifying happens. Jake reaches over and wipes one of my tears away with his thumb. My heart starts up again. And then, before I even have time to think about what's happening, Jake is leaning in toward me. His lips are, like, *two inches* away from mine, and he's looking right into my eyes. Jake is going to kiss me! This is the moment I've been waiting for! The moment where Jake will tell me that he likes me only, not Emma, that he's been wanting to kiss me ever since that day with his skateboard.

"Samantha," he says softly, and I wonder if his heart is beating as fast as mine.

But then, just as he's about to lean in for the kiss, out of nowhere, a rap song starts playing. Which is kind of weird, seeing as how I always figured my first kiss would be set to something a little more romantic. And then I realize it's Jake's phone. His ringtone is a rap song.

He picks up his cell from the desk, and I catch a glance at the caller ID before he sends the call to voicemail. But it's too late. I saw who it was. Emma.

"Who was that?" I ask, trying to keep my voice even.

"No one," he says. Which is a complete *lie*, since I saw the caller ID and I know it was definitely not a no one, it was definitely a *someone*. But I don't say this. I just look at him and still kind of hope that maybe he might try to kiss me.

But there's a knock on his open door, and it's his mom, and she wants Jake to know that dinner is ready, and then she asks me if I'm going to stay. But I say no, because, hello, how embarrassing is it to think that I maybe almost kissed Jake and now his mom is asking me to stay for dinner?

"So, um, I guess I'll get going," I say once Jake's mom is back downstairs. "So that you can have dinner."

"Yeah," Jake says.

I grab my bag off the back of my chair. "Um, so, I'll see you in school tomorrow."

"See you in school tomorrow," Jake says. He grins and gives me a little wave. He's kind of acting like nothing happened. Is it possible that maybe I *imagined* the whole thing? That maybe Jake wasn't trying to kiss me, that maybe he was just reaching over me for something and his lips kind of came close to me by accident or something? How will I know? What if he thinks I didn't want to kiss him and so now he's never going to try again? Boys have very fragile self-esteem. That's one thing I've learned from watching Taylor and all the boys who flock around her.

If only Jake would give me a sign! Some kind of sign before I leave that would let me know! I mean a *real* sign. Not something ambiguous like what just happened. I decide to walk out of his room verryyy slowly, just in case Jake wants to say something to make the situation better or to clarify things. But he doesn't say anything.

And then, right when I'm about to slip out the door, Jake finally speaks.

"Samantha?"

"Yeah?" I turn around, my heart soaring. He gets up and crosses the room, and for a second, I think that maybe he might try to kiss me again.

But instead, he holds his hand out. And when I look down, he's holding a note.

"Can you give this to Emma?" he says.

I take it. "Sure."

It's not a sign, it's not a sign, it's not a sign. That's what I tell myself as I stomp down Jake's stairs and out of his house. *It's not a sign, it's not a sign, it's not a sign.* That's what I tell myself as I walk home. *It's not a sign, it's not a sign, it's not a sign.* That's what I tell myself when I get up into my room and plop down on my bed, the note still in my hand.

It *can't* be a sign. Because it could say anything. They could be talking about anything! And unless I know for sure, I cannot jump to conclusions. But if I don't know for *sure*, how can I *not* jump to conclusions? I put the note down next to me on the bed. And then I pick it back up. And I know that this moment has been coming, it's been building, it's all been leading up to this.

So this time, I don't just almost kind of sort of break through the tape. This time, I open the note. For the first time in all of my secret-passing days, I read one of the secrets. Because I really just cannot take it anymore. And this time, I finally get my answer.

Because Jake's note to Emma only says one word. And that word is "yes."

thirteen

"IS THERE ANY POSSIBLE WAY THAT maybe he meant 'yes' about something totally random, like maybe she asked him if he's taking advanced math next year or something?" I know it's a stretch, but I'm desperate.

"No," Daphne says. It's the next morning, and we're hanging out outside near the side doors, waiting for the bell to ring for homeroom. Daphne has a soccer ball, and she's kicking it against the wall of the school. I'm supposed to be playing goalie, but I don't think I'm helping her practice all that much, because the ball just keeps going soaring by me. Pretty much every shot she takes is hitting the wall. I know I'm supposed to make it a little hard for her, but I might be the least coordinated person in the history of the world. Seriously.

"Is there any possible way that—"

"No," Daphne says. Another ball goes by me, and I reach down and pick it up, then toss it back to Daphne. "She was probably asking him if he liked her, or if he would go with her to the Fall Festival."

"Thanks," I say. Although I do have to give Daphne points for her honesty. At least I know she's not just telling me what I want to hear. That's why I haven't told her about how Jake and I almost kissed. I'm afraid she might tell me I really did just imagine it, and I'm so not ready to hear that.

"Look," she says. "If you want to do something about this situation, then you have to work with the facts. There's no use being in denial."

"True," I say. "But what can I do about it? There's no way I can compete with Emma."

"Yes, you can," she says. She pushes her bangs out of her face. "You haven't even *tried*. And besides, who cares about Emma anyway?" She makes a very disgusted face. "You're much better than Emma. You're prettier and smarter and nicer."

"I am *not* prettier than her," I say. Although the other things might be true. "And I don't know how to try," I say. "I don't want to actually have to go after Jake, I just want him to like me." I kick the ball back to Daphne, and she picks it up.

"Without even putting in any effort?"

"Yes," I say, nodding. "Without even putting in any effort." Daphne kicks the ball again. "Do you really think I'm prettier than Emma?"

"There you are!" Speak of the devil. Emma's voice comes trailing across the side of the school like nails on a chalkboard, and she comes waltzing into view. Today she's wearing a white button-down shirt and a pink and gray plaid wool skirt that flares around her knees, and there's a pink and gray beret perched on her head. Huh. I wonder where she got a matching beret-and-skirt set. Like, where does one buy such things? I hardly ever see berets when I'm out, much less berets with matching skirts. "I've been looking all over for you. I was at The Common for, like, at *least* half an hour waiting." She gives me an admonishing look.

"Why?" I frown. "We didn't have plans to hang out at The Common, did we?" I rack my brain, wondering if my maybe-real, maybe-imagined kiss has started to make me forget things.

"No, but you were there yesterday, so I figured that you would be there TODAY." Emma gives Daphne a big smile. "Hi, Daph."

"Hi," Daphne says tightly. She doesn't look too pleased.

"Anyway," Emma says. "Jake said he gave you a note for me."

I pull it out of my bag and hand it to her. She opens it, reads the "yes" and then smiles. If she notices anything weird about it (a.k.a. the fact that I had to tape it back up after reading it), she doesn't say anything. All she says is "Thanks. And, like, just so you know, I'm sorry we made you do all that secret-passing."

Made? As in past tense? "That's okay," I say, even though it's so totally not.

"I think Jake and I are at a point now where we'll probably just talk directly." She smiles again. "Oh! I totally forgot! Samantha, you owe me twenty dollars." She holds out her hand. I notice her nails are painted pumpkin spice, just like Taylor's. Must be the new fall trend.

"Twenty dollars? For what?" Good luck getting it, I think. I'm broke as a joke.

"For your cowboy hat," Charlie pipes up. She's walked up behind Emma. She's holding a to-go cup of something that looks hot, and she takes a dainty sip.

"Cowboy hat?" I sigh. "You guys, listen, I can't go as a wild cowgirl."

"But you have to!" Emma cries. "We already got three costumes. We can't go as two cowgirls; I told you that's lame!"

"We already started choreographing the dance,"

Charlie says, like the fact that they've already started coming up with a dance makes it impossible for me to not go. I guess she doesn't realize that a dance is going to dissuade me even more.

"Yeah," Emma agrees. "It goes like this." She starts jumping around, doing what I guess is supposed to be a line dance or something. But she kind of looks like one of those crazy Irish jig people who are always on TV around St. Patrick's Day. Emma has no idea she looks ridiculous, and she beams at me when she's done. "Isn't that awesome? We came up with it ourselves."

"You're going as a cowgirl to the Fall Festival?" Daphne asks. "With *them*?" She drops her soccer ball on the ground, and it goes rolling toward the school, where it bounces off the wall and into a puddle.

"No," I say firmly.

"*Yes*," Charlie says. "And so you owe us twenty dollars for the hat. Now give it."

"I thought the hats were free," I say. "The ones we tried on at your aunt's." Also, "give it"? Who says that?

"You were trying on things at *their aunt's house*?" Daphne shrieks.

"No," I say. "I mean, yes. I mean, no, not her house, we were at this costume shop, it was—look, it wasn't because I was going to go with them."

"You can be a cowgirl too, Daphne," Charlie says. "I'm sure we can find another costume."

"But I don't want to be a cowgirl," Daphne says.

"Sure you do," Charlie says. She takes another sip of her drink. "Wait until you see the costumes, they are so totally ah-mazing."

"So if you could bring us the money for the hat tomorrow, that would be great. And you too, Daph." Emma waves at us. "Toodles." And then she and Charlie disappear into school.

Daphne looks at me, her green eyes accusing.

"I'm not," I say, "going as a cowgirl."

"Sounds kind of like you are," she says.

"Well . . ." I drag my toe in the dirt pile near the bench, watching the mark my ballet flat makes. "It could be kind of fun. We could bring a cowbell or something."

"Yeah," Daphne says. "Maybe." She opens her mouth, like maybe she wants to say something else. But the bell rings then, and so she just picks up her soccer ball, wipes it off, and heads into school.

I'm not sure if it's my imagination or not, but it seems like maybe Jake is avoiding me.

Not, like, *avoiding* me avoiding me, but maybe just *kind of* avoiding me.

Case in point:

Wednesday, a summary: Homeroom: Jake says hi, but then buries himself in a skateboarding magazine and does not talk to me. Emma tries unsuccessfully to engage him in conversation (so maybe it's not just me?). Later, after sixth period, I say hi to him as he passes by me in the hall. He says hi back, but doesn't sound all that thrilled about it. There are no secrets in my locker from him. Or from Emma. Or, um, from anyone else.

Thursday, a summary: See Wednesday.

Friday, a summary: See Wednesday and Thursday.

The weekend, a summary: Jake doesn't call, IM, text, or attempt contact in any way.

Needless to say, by the time Monday morning rolls around, I'm feeling pretty cranky. How can I be anything but, when we haven't talked about our almost-kiss? Am I crazy? Was it really all in my head? Does Jake hate me? Are we not friends anymore?

In other scandals, Barb is coming tomorrow, and I have not gotten any secrets to pass in, like, a week. *And,* to top it all off, as if my life wasn't enough of a complete disaster, this morning I had to give Charlie twenty dollars for that dumb cowgirl hat. Daphne did too. We didn't even *want* to, but we somehow ended up doing it anyway. Although I guess it's not that surprising, when you think about it. I mean, Daphne and I are really no match for those two.

During second period, I decide I'm so not in the mood to deal with Emma and Charlie (they love to spend study hall passing notes, covertly watching videos on their iPhones, and gossiping—I can never get any work done), and so I head to the library, where I log in to one of the school computers to check my email.

Two new messages! Both from girls who were on the list of *You Girl* finalists! When I hadn't heard from anyone right away, I'd kind of given up on the idea that anyone was going to come through with an extra ticket. I cross my fingers and open the first email.

It's from the Darfur Girl. Greeeat.

Dear Samantha,

I am sorry it took me so long to get back to you. I put your email in my pending file, and as you can probably imagine, things have been sooo busy around here, and it took me a while to get to it. Orders for my FREEDOM bracelets have tripled in the past few weeks, and I've also started a new LIBERTY bracelet line. Feel free to check out my website, linked below, and pass it along to any of your friends you think might be interested.

Unfortunately, I don't have another ticket for the banquet. I am surprised you would think it was okay to put out a mass email like that, asking for one. As you know, being chosen as one of the You Girl finalists is a big honor, and it's not fair to expect someone to give up their ticket because YOU want to invite two people. A lot of people want to invite two people. In fact, I have about ten or eleven people who are just dying to come and support me.

Looking forward to seeing you at the dinner!
Love,
Candace
www.candace4darfur.com

Ugh, ugh, ugh. I really might hate that girl.

The other email is from Nikki, the girl at the photo shoot who helped me with my lip liner that day.

Hey Samantha,
Nice to hear from you. I'm sorry I took so long to write you back, I actually don't use this email address that much. (I gave it to You Girl just in case they decided to spam me with offers for their magazine—I know, I'm sneaky.)

If you still need an extra ticket, I have one. I'm

coming to the dinner by myself, since unfortunately my mom can't afford to take time off from work. Do you want to meet in the lobby before the dinner and I'll give you the ticket?

I'll have a You Girl escort with me, since I'm traveling by myself. (Can you tell how excited I am about that? Not.)

Hope to hear from you soon,

Nikki XXX

Oh my God, oh my God, oh my God! Yes, yes, yes, yes! An extra ticket! Which means both of my dads can go! Of course, I'm going to have to do some major convincing in order to get my dad to sit at the same table as Tom. But how much can he really protest? I mean, it's *my* night. So he kind of has to go along with what I want, doesn't he? Plus it's not like he even has to talk to Tom. He can just sit there and enjoy his dinner of roast chicken or whatever ridiculous thing they're serving and wait for the winner to be announced. Which will not be me, but that's a whole other story that will need to be dealt with later.

Yes, yes, yes! I wonder what I should wear. Probably something professional-looking. But not too professional, and definitely shoes with—

"Are you Samantha Carmichael?" a voice is saying. And, like, right in my ear, too—whoever it is has never definitely heard of personal space. I turn my head slowly to see a girl standing behind me. She has long blond hair, all the way down to her waist, and she's wearing a short white tiered skirt and earrings that are so big they brush against her shoulders.

"What?" I ask dumbly.

"Are you," she repeats, "Samantha Carmichael?" She taps her foot on the floor, and puts her hands on her hips.

"Yes," I say, before realizing that I probably should have figured out who she was and what she wanted before I told her who I was.

"Well, I'm Olivia Snetski," she says, real haughty-like. "Of Olivia's Secrets?"

"Oh. Uh, hi." The elusive Olivia! After that one day when I overhead her in the library, we haven't had any more run-ins. At first I was desperate to get her pointed out to me, but after a while, I kind of forgot about it. I didn't want to put a face to the business, I guess.

"I just wanted to say I am soooo sorry for ruining your whole company. I heard you're, like, devastated by it." She flips her long hair over her shoulder and gives me a sympathetic smile. And not in a nice way.

"You didn't *ruin* my whole business," I say. "But thanks for your concern." That's kind of (okay, a lot of) a lie, but Olivia doesn't know that. Does she? I guess she might. People might have told her that they're using her now instead of me. Plus she's probably getting so many secrets that she can't possibly imagine there could be any more out there. "And I'm not devastated by it." Another big lie.

"Yeah, well, that's not what everyone's saying." Olivia puts her hand on the back of my chair. French manicure. I guess she hasn't heard about the pumpkin spice craze.

"Who's everyone?" I ask.

"Just, you know, everyone." She smiles again. "Anyway, I just wanted to introduce myself so that things wouldn't be awkward between us. And if I ever need an assistant, I'll totally keep you in mind." She squeezes my shoulder in pity, waves her French manicure at me, and then walks away.

I stare after her, my mouth open. The nerve! I turn back to the screen, tears pricking at the backs of my eyes. Who am I kidding? Planning my outfit for the banquet next week, thinking about cute shoes? It's over. That lady Barb is coming tomorrow and it's going to be disastrous and everyone is going to find out I'm a fraud, including that jerk Olivia. Ugh, ugh, ugh. I log out of my email and head back to study hall. I might as well gossip with Emma and Charlie. No way I'm going to be getting any work done after *that*.

After school, I head to The Common to drown myself in doughnuts and a hot cider. Daphne's staying after for newspaper, so I'm going to work on homework until she's done, and then my mom's going to pick us up. Of course, I end up doing more obsessing over Barb's visit than homework, and so by the time Daphne comes marching into The Common after her meeting, I've only done two measly math problems.

Daphne has Karissa Green in tow. Like, she is literally holding Karissa's hand and pulling her toward the table I'm sitting at. I don't know Karissa that well—we have a few classes together, and we went to the same elementary school, but we're not close or anything.

Honestly, I'm a little annoyed. This morning I finally told Daphne about my maybe near-miss kiss and the fact that Jake is totally avoiding me, and I was hoping we could discuss (read: obsess about) it. But we can't do that in front of Karissa.

"Hi," Daphne says. She looks excited. Like, really

excited. She's about two steps away from jumping up and down and clapping her hands.

"Um, hi," I say. I try to send her a message with my eyes. The message being, you know, that I'm not in the mood for extra company. Karissa doesn't say anything. She just pulls at the bottom of her T-shirt.

"Hi, Karissa," I say. Now that she's here, I guess I at least have to try and be nice to her. "Do you want some doughnut?" I hold up my half-eaten glazed.

"Tell her," Daphne says proudly. She puts her hand on the small of Karissa's back and pushes her toward me.

Karissa's blue eyes look back and forth between me and Daphne nervously. "It's okay," Daphne says, sounding exasperated. "She's not going to *tell* anyone, she's a professional secret-keeper." I think about maybe adding "used to be," but decide to keep quiet.

"Okay, well." Karissa looks down at the ground. "I like Micah Wilkins."

"Oh," I say. "Well, that's great." I don't get it. Not to sound horribly mean, but who cares? I mean, Micah Wilkins? I know nothing about him, really, except that he's one of the cutest guys in our class. He went to Kennedy, but everyone at our school already knows who he is and loves him. He plays, like, every single sport and he has hair on his legs and wears a different pair of sneakers every day. I guess he's good-looking. Of course, Jake is way hotter, even if everyone else doesn't realize it.

"And . . . ," Daphne prompts, like a teacher trying to get their student to give the right answer.

"*And,*" Karissa says, "I sent him a secret through Olivia's Secrets asking him if he would go to the Fall Festival with me."

"That's very brave of you," I say generously.

"*And . . . ?*" Daphne says. She sounds *really* impatient this time. She's even tapping her foot on the ground.

"And now I'm not going with him," Karissa says. She sighs and rolls her eyes.

Daphne, apparently sick of waiting and pulling the story out of Karissa, decides to take over. "And the reason she's not going with him is because that jerk Olivia totally asked Micah after she read Karissa's secret!"

"What?!" I gasp, putting down my doughnut. Suddenly the story is getting interesting. I mean, way to bury the lead. I hope Daphne knows that if she wants to be a journalist, she's going to have to make sure she gives people the pertinent and interesting facts right off the bat.

"I know!" Daphne says. "I mean, Olivia totally asked him, like, ten minutes after you sent the secret, isn't that true, Karissa?"

"Yeah," Karissa says. She looks sad as she pulls on the bottom of her T-shirt some more. But then she says, "Whatevs, it doesn't matter anyway, because Micah really isn't as cute as everyone thinks he is. He's getting a mustache." She wrinkles up her nose when she says "mustache," like she can't even fathom how disgusting it is.

"And besides," I say, my heart sinking, "It doesn't prove anything. It could just be a coincidence."

"She definitely read it," Karissa says.

"How do you know?" I ask.

"Well, because I kind of said something cute to him in the note," Karissa says. "Something about how maybe if things worked out at the Fall Festival, we'd be doing more than just pumpkin picking." Her cheeks get all red. Wow. I had no idea Karissa had it in her to flirt like that. Maybe she should take my place and be the third crazy cowgirl.

"You mean you were implying that you guys would, like, kiss," Daphne clarifies.

"Right, but how do you know that Olivia definitely read the note?" I ask.

"Well, because I hadn't heard anything from Micah. And so I asked Olivia if she'd given him the secret, and she said yes."

"So . . ." God, this is like pulling teeth.

"*So*, finally I went up to Micah and I was all, 'Look, do you want to go to the Fall Festival or not; I sent you a secret and I know you got it and if you're trying to play hard to get, that's so not cool, because we're going to have to coordinate our costumes or whatever,'" Karissa says.

"Good for you," Daphne says. I nod. I mean, seriously. You have to give the girl some credit for having the guts to confront him.

"So *then* he says, 'Sorry, but I'm going with Olivia,' and so then I marched up to Olivia and was like, 'Did you ask Micah to the Fall Festival?' and she was all, 'Yeah why?' like super innocent." Karissa sighs. "Honestly, she might be the most annoying girl ever."

"That's what you get for not going through Samantha," Daphne says. She puts her arm around me and gives me a hug. "She's the best."

"So then what?" I ask Karissa.

"So then as I'm walking away, I hear her say to her friends, 'So, yeah, I'm going with Micah, and we might do more than pumpkin picking, if you know what I mean.'" She looks at me, a scandalized expression on her face. "In other words, she totally took what I was saying in my note and passed it off as her own. That's total *plagiarism*."

"Totally," Daphne agrees.

"Totally," I say, even though it kind of isn't. I think it's just more like copying.

"Anyway," Karissa says, sighing. "Next time I'll definitely go through you, Samantha." She gives us both a sad smile and then walks away.

"Wow," I say once she's out of earshot. "Olivia really *is* reading the secrets." A jolt of guilt flashes through me for a second, as I think about how *I* read a secret too. The one from Jake to Emma. The one that said "Yes." But that was only one! And it was totally under special, specific circumstances. Circumstances that any sane person would have caved under. And after a whole year of not reading ANY secrets, wouldn't you think that maybe a person would have the right to read one secret? One measly little secret? One measly little secret that didn't even tell the person anything, except for that fact that it said "Yes," which could mean anything??? Besides, I totally got what I deserved—mental torture and anguish. Plus I was basically fired from being their secret-passer and now Jake and Emma are just talking to each other all the time without me.

God, I really need another doughnut.

"She totally is," Daphne says. She reaches into her bag and pulls out an oatmeal cookie. "You want a bite?"

"No thanks," I say.

She puts her cookie down and turns her chair toward me. "So I was thinking about the whole cowgirl thing. And I've decided I'm on board."

"You're on board?" I ask.

"Yeah."

"With the whole cowgirl thing?"

"Yes," Daphne says. "That's what I just said!" She rolls her eyes. "I mean, I know I said I was before, but now I really am. I think it could be fun. And we'll be together, so even if Emma and Charlie are acting crazy, we'll have each other."

"Yes!" I say. "Exactly. We can maybe even ditch them and have fun on our own. We can probably even drive over without them. It's Saturday, so my mom will be off work, she can totally pick us up."

"It's Friday," Daphne says.

"What is?"

"The Fall Festival."

"What?!" Oh no, oh no, oh no. "But the *You Girl* banquet is on Friday!" I say.

"What?!" Daphne screeches, then throws her cookie onto the table. She glares at me.

"I totally mixed up the days!" I say. "You know I'm horrible with that stuff." It's true. I am horrible with that stuff. Once I almost forgot my own birthday. It was super embarrassing—my mom had this whole special breakfast planned with chocolate chip pancakes (my fave) and when I came downstairs I was all, "What's the occasion?"

"You forgot the date?" Daphne repeats incredulously.

"I am so, so sorry," I tell her. "And if you don't want to go with Charlie and Emma alone, seriously, you don't have to. Just tell them you don't want to go." God, this sucks. I mean, can this day get any worse?

"But I *do* want to go to the Fall Festival," she says. "I think it's going to be really fun."

"So then you can still go with them," I say. "It *will* be fun!" I'm trying to cheer her up and be a good friend, but the truth is, I'm pretty bummed, since (a) I really wanted to go, and (b) the thought of the three of them having fun without me is pretty upsetting.

"But it won't be the same." She kicks the table.

"I know, but—"

"Um, *hell*-o!" Taylor's voice comes echoing through The Common, and I do a double take. Taylor doesn't belong at The Common. She doesn't even belong at our *school*. But there she is, standing in front of us in her perfectly faded jeans and her black North Face jacket, tapping one Ugg boot on the ground impatiently. Her arms are crossed over her chest.

"Taylor!" I say. "What are you doing here?"

"Um, picking you up?" she says, like it's obvious. "What do you think? Mom and I have been waiting outside for, like, fifteen whole minutes. You weren't answering your cell." She plops down in the chair across from me. "Mom had to send me in here to get you. She went to get a coffee and she'll be back in a few minutes." She looks around The Common distastefully, like she can't believe she's back at the middle school. "So what are you guys talking about? You both have weird looks on your faces." Her tone implies that it can't be anything too interesting, since we're too young to have anything really worth talking about. If only that were the case.

"We're talking," I say, "about how horrible everything is." I put my head down on the table in frustration. Eww. Kind of sticky. I pull my head back up quickly.

"What could possibly be so horrible?" Taylor asks. She reaches over and takes a bite of Daphne's cookie. "You're in seventh grade."

"Shows how much you know," I tell her. Then I start ticking everything off on my fingers. "One, the Fall Festival is the same night as the *You Girl* dinner. Two, that woman Barb is coming tomorrow and I haven't gotten any secrets in weeks." I hesitate, contemplating going for three, but then decide to leave out the stuff about Jake.

"So what's going to happen?" Taylor asks, picking up my cider and taking a swig. "When she shows up and there aren't any secrets?"

"I'm not sure," I say. "Probably something completely and totally disastrous." I take the last bite of my doughnut and pop it into my mouth. I look at Taylor and Daphne. "Anyone have a brilliant plan?"

"Are you kidding?" Taylor asks. "I mean, isn't it so totally obvious?" Daphne and I look at her blankly. Taylor sighs like she can't believe how childish we are. "Samantha, all you have to do is make up some fake secrets."

"Fake secrets?" I ask skeptically.

"Yeah, like, just make up a whole bunch of fake ones and put them in your locker," Taylor says, shrugging. "That way, when that Barb person comes, she'll just think you have tons of them. She doesn't know anyone at your school, so she won't be able to tell that they're fake. You could even use real names."

"I don't know," I say. My stomach flips thinking about it. "What if I get caught?"

"Oh, please," Taylor says. She takes another long gulp of my cider, and I reach over and take it back from her before she drinks the whole thing. "You worry too much about things."

"I do?" I ask. I actually think I've been handling this whole situation quite well. I mean, my whole business is falling apart, not to mention that tomorrow a national magazine is coming to do a story about said falling-apart business, and somehow I'm still managing to keep it together. By a hair, but still.

"She might be right," Daphne says slowly. "Remember that time in fourth grade when me you and Jake needed money to go to the movies, because our parents wouldn't give us any, so we gathered up all the unopened food we could find in our houses and sold it and pretended we were raising money for the troops?"

"Exactly," Taylor says. "You didn't get caught that time, and you won't get caught this time either." She leans back in her chair and looks smug.

"You guys," I say. "That was fourth grade. We were *ten*. This is a little more serious."

"True," Daphne says. "If you get caught you'll probably get in a lot of trouble."

"God, you guys are, like, so *nervous*," Taylor says, sounding exasperated. She leans back in her chair, then reaches up and slides her hair tie out. Her long hair pools around her shoulders in soft waves. A couple of eighth-grade boys at the table next to us are staring at her, like, almost drooling.

"I don't know," I say. "I just . . . I don't think I can do that. I'm going to have to come up with something better."

"Suit yourself," Taylor says, shrugging.

"I *will* come up with something else," I say, nodding determinedly. "I *will.*"

fourteen

BUT I DON'T COME UP WITH ANYTHING else. Not One. Single. Thing. And by the time breakfast rolls around on Tuesday morning, I have a pit in my stomach the size of a cantaloupe.

"Oohh," I say from my seat at the kitchen table. "I don't fee-eeel so good." The one idea I *have* come up with is to fake sick. If I'm not at school when Barb comes, she can't figure out that my secret-passing is a sham, and voilà, perfect plan. Well, sort of. First I have to get Tom to let me stay home.

"What's wrong?" Tom asks, looking alarmed. He leaves the oatmeal he's making on the stove, and comes over and puts his hand on my head. "Are you getting swine flu?"

"Yes," I say. This was not something I really thought

of, but swine flu it is! "I'm getting swine flu. Someone at school told me their uncle had it, and I was hanging out with her a lot." This isn't even a lie. Someone at school *did* tell me her uncle had it. Of course, her uncle lives in South Dakota and was nowhere near the girl in question ever, but Tom doesn't need to know that. Also I don't think anyone even really gets swine flu anymore, and if they do, it gets knocked out with an antibiotic in, like, five seconds. Unless you have one of those rare, serious cases. Which I obviously do.

"Swine flu is totally going around," Taylor says, coming into the kitchen. "And if you have it, please don't get near me, since it's going to be homecoming soon."

"I won't get near you," I promise. I decide that if Tom thinks this new swine flu development is pretty serious, then I should start acting it. Plus I heard somewhere that serious swine flu can progress rapidly. "Oooh, my head," I say, resting it on the table.

The phone rings then, and Tom reaches over me to get it.

"Hello? Hello? Oh, yes, hi, Richard. . . . Yes, she's right here. Unfortunately, she's not feeling well; we think it might be swine flu." Tom turns around to stir the oatmeal.

Gasp! Tom is on the phone with my dad! Talking

about how I have swine flu. I don't think that's going to go over so well. My dad is probably expecting me to be at school no matter what, even if I have, like, rubella or something. Not that I know what rubella is. I just know that it's pretty bad, since you have to get vaccinated for it. Anyway, the point is, a little bout of swine flu is not going to be enough for my dad to think it's okay for me to miss my time with Barb.

"Well, I know today is the day that *You Girl* is coming to her school, but if Samantha's sick, then that takes precedence over— No, I will *not* ask her if she's faking, that is not a very nice thing to even *imply*; Samantha would *never*— Why, yes, maybe you should call her mother on her cell phone, that might be a better—Hello? Hello? HELLO?"

Tom hangs up the phone and looks at it in wonder. "Your father," he says, "just hung up on me."

Taylor and I look at each other nervously. Hmm. This probably isn't the best time to bring up the fact that they're both going to the *You Girl* dinner.

"Oooh," I say. "My throat is really hurting."

"Do you want some oatmeal?" Tom asks. "Or maybe I should make you some soup."

"Yes, oatmeal, please." Tom makes the best oatmeal. He puts nuts and apples and all sorts of good things into it. "And then I'd better get upstairs to bed; I think maybe I'm going to have to cancel today. Now where's Barb's number?" I grope around the table for my cell phone. I'm hoping Tom will offer to call Barb for me, since I'm slightly scared of her.

"See how you feel once you get something in your stomach," Tom says. Taylor rolls her eyes and pulls two bowls down from the cupboard. She's obviously caught on to the fact that I'm faking. She also knows that Tom is a total pushover, and that if I want to stay home from school, I'll be able to. As long as my mom doesn't find out.

"So what are your symptoms exactly?" Taylor asks. "Because I heard that if it's really swine flu, you'll have a really bad fever."

"I *do* feel hot." I start fanning myself with the newspaper that's sitting on the table.

Taylor raises her eyebrows at me skeptically. "Then you probably shouldn't eat oatmeal, you should have cool things. Like orange juice."

I glare at her. Taylor knows that I hate orange juice. My mom always buys the kind with the pulp, and there are always little bits of orange floating around in there. Yuck, yuck, yuck.

"I need something warm to soothe my throat," I say. I rub my throat for good measure.

Tom plunks a bowl of oatmeal down in front of me, and another in front of Taylor. I take a warm, sweet spoonful. Yum.

"This is so good," I say. "But, um, not so good that I'm feeling better or anything."

"Of course not," Taylor says, rolling her eyes again. She takes a bite of her own oatmeal.

And then my mom comes into the kitchen. "Mom!" I say, shocked. "What are you doing here?" My mom is not supposed to be home right now. It's only seven thirty. My mom gets out of work at nine a.m. Also, it is impossible to get a hold of my mom, because she is an ER nurse and when you call her, there are all sorts of things going on, like shootings and stabbings. Actually, not really. Mostly it's just people who broke their legs in skiing accidents or kids with appendicitis. But she's still usually really busy dealing with important things that do not allow her to get to the phone. Which was an integral part of my swine flu plan.

"I got out of work early," she says. "I've been upstairs since five, catching up on the DVR."

I look at Tom. "Tom," I say accusingly. "Did you know about this?"

"Of course."

"You could have told me," I mumble. Now that my

mom is here, there's no way I'm going to be allowed to stay home from school. Which really sucks, especially since I just got my hopes up, and now they are dashed into oblivion.

"Samantha has swine flu," Taylor reports.

"I heard." My mom crosses the kitchen, pulls a bowl down from the cupboard, and fills it with oatmeal from the pot on the stove. "Do you have a fever?"

Crap, crap, crap. This is why it's not so great to have your mom be a nurse. Sure, it comes in handy *sometimes* like when you fall off a swing in second grade and become convinced you're going to bleed to death because there is blood everywhere and you are afraid it means you're going to die. Then your mom can just pick you up and you can trust her when she says it just needs a Band-Aid, because she's a medical professional.

But when you are in seventh grade and pretending to have swine flu, it's a whole different story.

"I don't think I have a fever," I say. "But one might be developing."

"Hmm." She puts her cool hand to my forehead.

"Your hand feels so very cold," I try.

"Yes, well, you don't have a fever," she says.

"But you can't tell if someone has a fever just by

feeling their forehead! I read it online, it was a breaking news story on my AIM!"

"Samantha," she says. "You're not sick. You're going to school. Your father and I talked about it, and really, there's nothing you need to be worried about. You're going to do fine."

Easy for them to say. They don't have all the information.

Two hours later, I'm sitting in the front office waiting for Barb. She's late. I don't think this is a very good way to start our day. And I think it's very unprofessional of Barb to be late, but honestly, I can't say anything, because she holds my fate in her hands. Also, I can't *really* talk about people being unprofessional. Because this morning, before school started, I met Daphne at The Common and we made up a bunch of fake secrets, which I then shoved into my locker. I know. It's totally shameful. But I didn't know what else to do! And when you think about it, it's not *really* a lie. Because as soon as Olivia gets sick of this whole thing, my business will be back on track. So really I'm just sort of messing around with the timing.

"Did she call or anything?" I ask Mrs. James, the front-office secretary.

"No, hon," she says, shrugging. "If she's not here by the time first period is over, we'll let you go to class and just call you down when she gets here."

Ooh, score! If that happens, I can just be all, *I'm so sorry, Barb, but since you were late, I have a very important test that, unfortunately, I just cannot miss.* And then I'll let her take a pic of me or something, so that at least she doesn't go away completely empty-handed. And then I'll tell her I understand that she doesn't have much information to really make a good profile, but that my education is more important, and that I hope she can respect that. What a good speech!

I watch the clock over the office door tick toward the end of first period, when I can make my escape. The good news, I guess, is that I'm missing first period. I look down and smooth my skirt. I'm wearing a black pencil skirt, a white lacey shirt, and a gray and maroon sweater with matching patterned tights. Very cute outfit. Too bad it will be all for nothing since Barb isn't coming, yay!

And then, literally *right before* the bell is going to ring, Barb comes barging into the office. She just walks right in, she's got a photographer(!!) in her wake, and she looks like she's on a mission.

She rings the bell that's sitting on the desk of the front

office, even though Mrs. James is sitting right there.

"Yes, hello," she says. *Ding, ding, ding.* "I'm dreadfully sorry that I'm so tardy, but I'm here to see Miss Samantha Carmichael." She narrows her eyes and peers at Mrs. James over these really small wire spectacles that she's wearing. "We're doing a story for *You Girl*, and I've already cleared it with your principal."

"Yes, I know," Mrs. James says. She doesn't sound too happy. "Samantha is sitting right over there, where she's been waiting for you and *missing class* since you said you'd be here forty-five minutes ago."

"Samantha!" Barb says, ignoring Mrs. James's snarky remark and rushing over to me. "It is so nice to finally make your acquaintance."

"Nice to make yours as well." I extend my hand, and she shakes it. For a second, I feel like maybe I'm supposed to curtsy or something. But I don't, I just stand there. It's a little awkward, honestly.

Finally, I put my hand out to the photographer. "Hi," I say. "I'm Samantha Carmichael."

He takes my hand, but doesn't say anything.

"Tony is just here to snap a few photographs for the profile, and for our slide show at the banquet." Barb looks at him with distaste. I think it might be because he's wearing jeans and a pair of dirty sneakers. Honestly, he's not much of a camera crew. Not that I mind. The fewer cameras the better.

Barb leans in and whispers to me, "He doesn't work for *You Girl*, he's just *freelance*." She says "freelance" like it's some kind of really dirty word.

"Oh, okay." I'm not sure what to say about that. Tony just grunts again.

"Anyway!" Barb says. "Moving on! So! It's best to just relax and seem natural as we shadow you this morning. Don't get too focused on the camera. Tony will take your picture throughout the next hour or so, but just try to ignore him."

"Okay," I say. As if on cue, Tony snaps a pic. I blink in surprise at the flash. "Oh, um, sorry." I smooth my skirt and try to recover. "I, uh, didn't know you were going to take a picture."

"They're candids," Barb explains. "You won't know when he's going to take them." She turns to Tony. "Samantha's a blinker," she says. "So we have to be careful that we make the pictures look candid when they're not *really* candid."

"I'm not a blinker," I lie, mostly because it's embarrassing to be called a blinker. Also, what does she mean, make the pictures look candid when they're not? God, it's hot in here.

"Yes, you have the characteristics of a blinker," Barb says. And then she pulls a magazine proof sheet out of her bag. "Here you are, see? Page sixty-eight, Samantha Carmichael, secret-passer."

She hands it to me. I gasp. There I am, at the photo shoot they did that day, and I don't look so great. I *am* slightly blinking, and one of my eyebrows is a little bit higher than the other, so that it looks like I'm trying to give the camera a knowing look.

"Why did they pick *that* picture?" I ask before I can stop myself. "There must have been better ones!"

"I don't know," Barb says. "But don't get your tights all bunched up; no one cares about what you look like." She gives me a disapproving look, like I shouldn't be worried about what I look like in a national magazine that is going to be seen by millions of people. She holds the sheet out to me. "Here you go!" she says. "You can keep the proof. The magazine won't be out on newsstands until next month."

"Great," I say, sliding it into my bag. Maybe they'll put a really good picture of me into the profile they're doing, something that will make up for the fact that this picture sucks. Maybe everyone else's pictures look really bad too, like they wanted us all to look a little bit dorky so that the readers would relate to us. Not that *You Girl*'s readers are dorky. I mean, *I* read *You Girl*.

"Now!" Barb claps her hands, and I jump. "Please show us to your locker, Samantha." Tony snaps another picture.

"Okay," I say. I wave goodbye to Mrs. James, who gives me a sympathetic smile (she totally knows that Barb is crazy), and start leading them down the hall toward my locker. The problem is that my locker isn't that close to the main office, so we have kind of a long walk.

"Well, this is my school," I say, because I can't just say nothing. Tony snaps a picture and then grins. I concentrate on making sure my eyes are open. I'm not sure if I'm succeeding.

"It's a very nice school," Barb says. "You wouldn't believe some of the institutions we've had to visit." She shudders.

"Oh, yeah, that must have been hard." How snobby. "That's the cafeteria," I say as we pass. "Before and after school, they call it The Common Ground, but we call it The Common for short. Anyway, uh, they sell hot chocolate and muffins and stuff, and we get together and study." Tony snaps a pic of it, but Barb wrinkles up her nose.

"Do they offer healthy, organic meals?"

"Well, not really. They do have some soy muffins, though. My friend Daphne loves them."

"Hmm." Barb makes a mark in the notebook she's carrying. "That would be a great idea for some entrepreneurial young mind. Start a cart in their school that carries organic, free-trade food and drinks for those students who are concerned about their health."

She gives me a pointed look. And it could totally be because I'm overthinking things, but I have a feeling she might mean that once I get over all this silly secret-passing ridiculousness, I should maybe do something important, like sell organic foods.

"Well, here we are!" I say. "This is where all the magic happens!" That's a very dorky thing to say, but for some reason, it just pops out.

"This is where you receive your secrets, correct?" Barb steps close to the locker and inspects the vent. "You're lucky that the locker has a vent. Otherwise what would your business do?"

"Yes, well, I organized my business around the fact that lockers have vents. I, uh, researched a few different methods of secret-dropping-off, and I figured lockers were the most logical structure."

Barb nods, impressed, even though obviously I just made that whole thing up.

"Get a picture of her in front of her locker," Barb instructs.

Tony snaps another one. I try to remember to keep my eyes open.

"Now," Barb says. "You could . . ." She trails off, and her eyes focus on something above my head. "What's that?"

"What's what?" I ask, smoothing my hair down.

"*That?*"

I turn to see what she's pointing at. Uh-oh. One of Olivia's flyers. Right over *my* locker! Ugh. I mean, *really.*

"Oh, that," I say, waving my hand like it's no big deal. "That's nothing, that's just . . . some girl at school thought it would be fun to start her own secret-passing business when she heard about mine. And so, ah, that's one of her flyers."

"Hmm," Barb says. "Interesting." She adjusts her spectacles and leans in for a closer look.

"Not really," I say. "I mean, she *obviously* doesn't realize what goes into a business, how totally *committed* you really have to be to make it successful." I smooth my skirt again and keep going. "The problem with a lot of kids these days is that they don't realize that being an entrepreneur is a lot of work. Yes, you can make it happen, but you have to be willing to put in the time." This is a line I totally memorized just for this occasion. But Barb doesn't have to know that. I want her to think I sound smart, like, off the cuff.

Barb's scribbling something down on her clipboard. "You can quote me on that if you want," I offer.

"Samantha, this is interesting, the idea of competing businesses going on in a middle school. Would you say that our need for the free market and antitrust laws dribbles down into even middle school businesses?"

"Well, I wouldn't say that exactly." Honestly, I have no idea what she's talking about.

"What do you mean?" Barb asks.

"What do I mean about what?"

"About the antitrust laws? You said 'not exactly,' what does that mean?"

"Well, all I really mean is that so far, this other business hasn't really affected me. I'm much more established than Olivia; I have a very *loyal* clientele."

I decide this whole interview is starting to get away from me, and needs to end pretty much as soon as possible. Plus I don't want her asking me any more hard questions about economic or foreign rights or whatever it is she's talking about. So I turn around and open my locker.

"You see?" I say. All the notes come tumbling out, some onto the floor. I did that on purpose, shoved them all in there so that they'd come falling out when I opened the door. It looks very impressive. "My business isn't suffering in the slightest!"

"Yes, I see that," Barb says. She beams. "Now, how many secrets do you have here?"

"Well, let's see," I say. I start picking them all up from the floor, even though I know that the exact number is twenty-three, since I'm the one who made them all.

"Looks like we have about . . ." I'm counting them up and gathering them into my arms when the bell rings, signaling the end of first period. All of a sudden, the hallway becomes filled with kids, all on their way to their next class.

"Who's this guy?" Ronald Hughes says as he rushes by. He puts his face right in front of Tony. "You gonna take my picture, man?" He laughs and then keeps walking.

"Ha-ha," I say. "That was just Ronald, he's very funny." Tony doesn't look too pleased.

"Oh my God, Samantha!" a voice yells. Great. Emma. Although maybe having a girl who looks and acts like Emma (always knows the right thing to say, looks very smart and put-together, definitely a little bit of a suck-up), will help me with Barb. Barb seems like the kind of person who would just love Emma. "I was looking all over for you! You, like, totally weren't in homeroom."

"Yes, I was," I say. "I just had to leave early."

"Oh, right, for your magazine thing." She turns to Barb and holds out her hand. "I'm Emma Clydell," she says. "I'm Samantha's best friend." Um, not really, but now's definitely not the time to bring *that* up.

"Nice to meet you," Barb says. "This is Tony." Tony grunts, and Emma gives him a nod, then flips her curly red hair over one shoulder.

"Anyway, Samantha, I need your money for our cowgirl outfits," Emma says. She looks at me expectantly.

"Your cowgirl outfits?" Barb asks.

"Samantha didn't tell you?" Emma asks.

"No," I say. "I didn't. That's not really Barb's specialty, if you know that I mean." I'm trying to let her know that it's probably not the best time to bring up the fact that I'm going to be dressing as a cowgirl on the night of the Fall Festival. What is wrong with her, anyway? I thought she was supposed to be good around adults. And then I remember. I still haven't told Emma I can't go to the Fall Festival. Well, no time like the present! Emma won't be able to freak out in front of Barb, and it will make me look super responsible. "Actually, Emma," I say, "it turns out that I can't go to the very fun Fall Festival. I'm so disappointed to miss it, but I have to honor my obligation and attend the *You Girl* banquet that night."

"But we were going to be cowgirls!" Emma whines. Her delicate features arrange themselves in a pout. "Charlie's even going to not wear a T-shirt under hers."

She turns to Barb. "I think it's ridiculous how certain costumes have been condemned by society just because a woman might be showing off a little bit of her body. If my friend Charlie wants to have a tiny little bit of her stomach showing, then she should be able to, right? *Boys* would be able to."

"Well, I'm not sure that would be appropriate for a school function," Barb says. She seems a little . . . miffed. Oh, God, oh, God, oh, God. Please do not let Barb write something down about this.

I give Emma another look. "Yes, well, we'll have to talk about it later," I say. "Barb and Tony are shadowing me and they have a limited amount of time."

"Well, okay," Emma says. But she doesn't look convinced. She turns to Tony. "Do you want to get a picture of me and Samantha? We could pose right under her locker, and you could put in the magazine that we're besties." She puts her arm around me and gives them a big smile.

"No," Barb says. "I don't think that will be necessary, but thank you."

"All right," Emma says. She lets go of me reluctantly. "Well, I guess I'll see you at lunch, Samantha."

"I guess so," I say. I let out the breath I've been holding. Now that Emma's going away, I can get this rodeo back on track. Or at least try to.

Emma takes one step down the hall, but her black patent leather shoe slips on something. "Oooh," she says, looking down. "What's this?" She crouches down and picks up the piece of paper that's under her shoe. One of the fake notes that was in my locker. One of the fake notes that was in my locker and has her name on it.

"Oh, that," I say. I reach out and grab it from her. "That was just a note that was in my locker."

"But it has my name on it."

"Right," I say. "So, you know, I'll give it to you later, when I'm doing my rounds." Which is a really dumb thing to say, since I don't do rounds, and Emma knows it.

"But I want to read it now," Emma says. She stamps her foot. "It could be from Jake."

"Oooh, this is perfect!" Barb claps her hands. "Samantha, you give Emma the note, and Tony will take a picture. A real action shot!"

"Uh, no," I say. "That's not really how it—"

"Samantha," Barb says, her voice steely. "Please do it."

What else can I do? I hold the note out to Emma, and she takes it. Tony snaps the picture.

"Okay," I say, giving her a pat on the back. "Off you go, off to second period!"

"But I hate second period," Emma says. She looks

at Barb. "The teacher is very boring." And then Emma opens her note. She frowns and flips it over. "It's totally blank." She looks confused. "I wonder if this is some kind of game Jake is playing. We're going to the Fall Festival together, and he said he was going to be a cowboy." She giggles. "So maybe, like, cowboys used to write with invisible ink or something? To fool the Indians?"

"We don't say Indians," Barb says automatically. "We say Native Americans."

"You're going to the Fall Festival with Jake?" My voice is barely above a squeak.

"Yeah," she says. "You're not mad that he's coming with me, are you? I still want to dress the same and everything, and we can still hang out there."

I don't even bother trying to explain to her again that I'm not going to the Fall Festival because (a) that would be fruitless, and (b) I'm having a hard time processing what is going on. One, Emma has opened a fake note in front of Barb, and two, she is going to the Fall Festival with Jake. *My* Jake! Jake who almost-kissed me last week, who has been listening to me and making excuses to hang out with me alone, and who promised he would figure out a way to hack into the Olivia's Secrets website. *And who's been kind of avoiding you,* a little voice in the back of my head whispers. I try to ignore that voice.

"So let me get this straight," Barb says. "Your note is blank? Do students often send blank notes?"

"Well—" I start, but Emma cuts me off.

"No," she says, peering down at the note thoughtfully. "It's very strange. Although it might have something to do with Olivia's Secrets. Did Samantha tell you what a huge pain in the butt that girl is being?"

"What Emma *means*," I say, "is that even though it's certainly not *standard*, often certain students do—"

But before I can finish what I'm saying, Tony bends down and picks up another note from the floor. He opens it. "It's blank," he says, speaking for the first time since he got here. And then he opens up two more. And then he looks up at Barb with a totally scandalized look on his face. "They're all blank," he says.

fifteen

BARB AND TONY HAVE TO STAY FOR
the rest of their time. It's very awkward, since obviously
Barb knows I planted those notes. She doesn't come
right out and say it, but she knows. She just doesn't have
any proof. By the time she leaves, I'm a mess. I feel like
crying, and I just want to go home. Somehow I make it
through the rest of my classes, but by the time the day's
over, I feel like my head's going to explode.

"Now, you stand here and kick the ball toward me,"
Daphne says. "And I'll be the goalie." After I filled Daphne
in on what happened today, she somehow conned me
into staying after to practice soccer with her. I totally
protested, but Daphne said it would keep my mind off
everything. So before I knew it, I was wearing cleats,
a pair of soccer shorts, and some kind of shin guards.

Which is very scary, since if you need to wear shin guards, that means your shins are in danger of something bad happening to them, and I really don't like that. I need my shins. They're important.

"Is goalie what you want to try out for?" I ask.

"I'm not sure," she says. "Maybe."

"How about I try to be the goalie?" I ask.

"But how will that help *me* to be the goalie?" Daphne wants to know. Daphne's wearing a similar outfit to mine, but she has on a sweatband, and she's drawn two black streaks under her eyes. She looks very hardcore.

"Um, because you'll get to see what it's like on the other side?" Of course, I just don't want to kick balls. Of course, on the other hand, getting balls kicked at me at what I assume are high speeds doesn't sound so great either.

"Nice try," she says, taking her place in between the two goalposts.

"Fine," I grumble. "Even though I'm the one who's having the most horrible life ever." I march a few yards away and set the ball down next to me. At least now I won't have balls flying at my face.

"Now give it a kick," she says. I don't really feel too much like kicking. I give it a kick, which turns out to be more like a soft tap. Hmm. Not so great. The ball rolls a few feet and stops well short of the goal.

"That's all you got?" Daphne says. She shakes her head and then says sadly, "I have a feeling we might be here for a while." And then her eyes look past me, out onto the field. "Uh-oh," she says, getting this sort of panicked look on her face.

"What?" I ask. And then I turn around and see Jake loping toward us across the grass, his computer bag slung over his shoulder and his baseball hat on backward. Figures that when I finally see him, I'm out of my super cute outfit and in my shorts and T-shirt. At least I opted out of putting that black paint under my eyes. Not that it matters. He's taking Emma to the Fall Festival, so what do I care what I look like?

"Hey," he says to me when he gets close. "I was looking for you."

I want to say something super smart and sarcastic like *Oh, now you're looking for me*, or *Why, is Emma busy?* But all I say is "Well, here I am." I cross my arms and wait. Wait for him to say something about how he's not really going to the Fall Festival with Emma, how it's all some kind of big mix-up. Or maybe something about how he almost-kissed me. Or how he's sorry for blowing me off for the past week. But all he says is "So how did it go today? With Barb?"

"Horrible!" I say, throwing my hands up in the air. We

haven't talked since our almost-kiss and *that's* the first thing he asks me?

"Really?" Jake asks. He sounds surprised. And there's something about that that starts to make me even madder than I already am. I mean, he would *know* how it went already if he hadn't been acting all weird. Rage courses through my body. I've been trying all day not to think about what Emma said. About her and Jake and the Fall Festival. I've been trying not to think about how Jake almost-kissed me and then asked *Emma* to go with him. I've been trying not to think about how they've passed covert notes through me, not even caring about *my* feelings or bothering to tell me what's in them. I've been trying not to think about what a COMPLETE AND TOTAL JERK JAKE IS. But now that he's here, right in front of me, I can't help thinking about all of these things.

"Yes," I say, "really. Which you would have known if you hadn't been ignoring me."

"I wasn't ignoring you," Jake says, and then gives a little laugh, like it's no big deal, like ha-ha, we'll laugh about this someday like the fourth-grade food-selling story, but I'm not in the mood to be brushed off. I narrow my eyes at him.

"Uh-oh," Daphne says from behind me. "Um, I'm going to go in and grab my cell," she says. "And call my mom to make sure she knows what time to come and pick us up."

"No," I say. "You don't have to go." If Daphne goes, that means we're definitely getting into a fight. And Jake and I are not fighting. We're just having a little discussion.

"It's not a big deal," Daphne says. "I'll come right back and then we can practice more." She takes off running toward the gym.

"Look," Jake says, taking a step toward me. "Listen, I wanted to tell you that I'm working on a new program. To try to hack into Olivia's website? Leo's older brother helped me with it, he thinks it could—"

"So, is it true about you and Emma?" I blurt.

"What?" His face goes a little pale.

"That you guys are going to the Fall Festival together?"

"Um, well . . ." He looks at me. "I mean, you're going to be at the *You Girl* banquet, right?"

"That's not the question."

"No," he says. "I mean, yeah, she asked me if I wanted to go, and I said I'd meet up with her there."

I look down at the ground. "Oh," I say. My head is suddenly spinning. Taylor *told* me this was going to happen. She would always say, "You know, when you get older, I bet you're going to start liking Jake." And my ten-year-old self would wrinkle up my nose and make a gagging noise, because Jake was my friend and boys were gross. But now . . . Now I *do* like him, and it just seems so unfair. I feel like my best friend is getting taken away from me, and there's nothing I can do about it. Everything's a mess.

Yes, a little voice whispers in the back of my head. Everything *is* a mess. But it's not Jake's fault. *You* got yourself into all of these situations. *You* read that secret and drove yourself crazy trying to figure out what it meant. *You* wanted to be friends with Charlie and Emma because they seemed cool and you wanted to be cool at your new school. *You* invited your dad and Tom to the banquet, and *you* made up those fake secrets. And most of all, you didn't just come out and tell Jake you liked him and you never asked him if he wanted to go to the Fall Festival with you, and what those almost-kisses meant.

"Excuse me," I say to Jake, picking up the soccer ball that's on the ground next to me. "I have to go get Daphne."

And this time, I'm really going to whip that ball.

When I get home, I head right upstairs to Taylor's room and knock on the door. I've decided that I've been going about this whole Olivia thing completely the wrong way, and so I need her advice. And yeah, Taylor's suggestion to make fake notes didn't work out so well, but she *is* good at coming up with ideas. I'll just have to make sure to pick and choose the ones that aren't too crazy.

"What?" she yells, her voice muffled and her music loud.

"I need you," I say, raising my voice to be heard over Taylor Swift. (Taylor's favorite artist, for obvious reasons.)

Taylor opens the door and looks me up and down. "Come in," she says. Like I said, Taylor can be a complete and total pain sometimes, but she's there when you need her.

"What's up?" She flops down on her bed, where she's doing something to her hair. Looks like putting it in tons of little braids with beads on the end.

"What are you doing?" I ask. I sit down next to her, and the pile of beads slides into the depression in the comforter. I pick them up and arrange them back into their neat pile.

"Putting tons of little braids with blue and white beads in my hair," she says, in a way that's like, *Duh.* "It's going to be homecoming soon, and so I'm practicing hairstyles for the pep rally."

Wow. I didn't even know you needed a separate hairstyle for the pep rally, much less that you needed to practice them. This is why I need Taylor. She knows things like this.

"So what's going on?" she asks. "I'm going over to Amanda's in a few, so spill."

"Well," I say slowly, dragging my hand through the bead pile and letting them fall through my fingers. Then I gather them all back up and do it again. "You're good at figuring things out about people, right?"

"What do you mean?" Taylor slides another blue bead up one of her braids, then ties it off with a tiny rubber band.

"Like gossip," I say. "You're good at getting gossip out about people."

"I guess," she says, shrugging.

"So what if," I say, "*hypothetically*, I wanted to expose someone, like figure out something bad they did?"

Taylor frowns and looks at me suspiciously. "You mean like a scandal from their past?"

"No," I say. "Something they're doing now. Like, maybe if they were, uh, participating in immoral business practices."

Taylor gives me a look. "Immoral business practices?" she asks. "Are you kidding me?"

"Fine," I say, rolling my eyes and putting it in simpler terms. "A girl started a rival secret-passing business and I think she's reading all the secrets."

"Oh," Taylor says, then shrugs like that's child's play. "Then you would follow her."

"Follow her?" Hmmmm. I never thought of that. "I never thought of that," I say.

She shrugs again. "It's kind of the best way. I mean, it's pretty easy to follow people without them knowing, if you're smart about it. Like, this time when we thought Amanda's boyfriend was cheating on her? We just trailed him from Subway to the bowling alley, and he was totally meeting up with Brianna Sullivan." She gets a disgusted look on her face. "Amanda had to break up with him of course. And we ruined our high heels walking so far, but we got the info we wanted."

"Thanks, T." I give her a hug. Following Olivia around is slightly shady, but it's not, like, illegal or anything. Plus what Olivia's doing is way worse. Not to mention stalking me down in the library.

"Wait!" Taylor says as I move to get off her bed. "That's it? You just come in here asking for stalking advice and then I don't even get to know any more of the deets?"

"We-ell," I say, settling back in. "So there's this girl, Olivia, right?" I fill her in on pretty much everything that's been going on.

"And have *you* considered building a website?" she asks when I'm done.

"Well, sort of," I say. "I mean, I *did* consider it for all of two seconds. But I don't have the money for that."

"If you don't have the money," she says. "You might have to think outside the box."

"Outside the box?"

"Yeah, like, Amanda totally can't afford to get her hair blown out for homecoming, but she's getting this girl we know who takes cosmetology to do it. And then she's going to lend her her green organza dress." She slides another bead up her braid. "Get it? Like a trade?"

"Taylor," I say. "I'm in seventh grade; I don't know anyone who makes websites." But then I remember. That's not really true. I *do* know someone. Nikki. The girl who's giving me her extra ticket to the *You Girl* banquet. I remember when we met at the photo shoot, she told me she was a website designer. Maybe I could get a cheap or reduced rate in exchange for putting her business name on the website!

"Taylor," I say, awed. "I think you might be a genius."

"Duh," she says. She looks at herself in the mirror. "Do you think these braids are a little much?"

Nikki's going to make me a website! I emailed her, and she called me right away, and she knows all about coding and stuff, and she said she'll only charge me a hundred dollars! Of course, with business being the way is, that's pretty much all the money I have. And I was totally saving it up for a Blu-ray player, or an iPhone, or maybe some new clothes. But I guess I'll just have to look at it as an investment in myself.

I'm so excited and motivated by the possibility of my website, that the next day at school, I put Operation Stalk Olivia into action. (Eric Niles works in the main office during his study hall, and he copied down her schedule for me.) I tail her to math. I tail her to science. I follow her into the library during her free period, and then try to see what she's doing at the computer. She almost catches me when I follow her into the bathroom between seventh and eighth periods. I thought she'd left, but when I come out of the stall she's still at the sink, drying her hands.

"Well, well, well," she says. "If it isn't Samantha Carmichael. I heard you put fake notes in your locker and then had to scramble when the *You Girl* lady caught you."

"Who told you that?" I ask nonchalantly.

"Wouldn't you like to know." She reaches into her purse and pulls out a pink lipstick, then lines her lips. The thing is, I kind of already know. Who told her, I mean. There are only four people in this whole world besides me who know what happened that day. Barb and Tony are, obviously, out, unless somehow they ran into

Olivia and decided to tell her. Not likely. No way Daphne would say anything. So that leaves Emma. Sigh.

"Not really," I say, shrugging. "It was probably Emma." I can tell by the look on her fact that I have it right. "And if there's any information I *really* want to know, it's why people think their secrets are being read."

I rip a piece of paper towel off of the holder, dry my hands, and then walk out.

By the end of the week (and the day of the *You Girl* banquet), I still have nothing on Olivia. Not one. Single. Thing. I've followed her all week, and I have absolutely *nothing* to show for it. Although, there was one small sliver of time today where I lost sight of her between third and fourth periods. I saw Jake coming down the hall, and I ducked into an empty classroom so I wouldn't have to pass him. She could have done something shady then. It's such a shame! It would have been absolutely perfect if I could have exposed her today, the day of the *You Girl* banquet. Of course, I have bigger problems, i.e., the fact that I still haven't told Tom or my dad that they're both going to the banquet. An it's in, um, three hours.

"Maybe she's not reading them," I wail to Daphne while we're sitting outside on the benches after school, sharing a bag of chips and waiting for Daphne's news-paper meeting to start.

"She definitely is," Daphne says. "We just have to think. What *did* you find out today?"

"Nothing!" I say. "Absolutely nothing, except that Olivia likes to reapply her lip gloss about three bajil-lion times a day. She's probably reading them at home. Which makes sense. I mean, think about it—the only ones she would read at school are the paper ones. And most of her secrets are probably digital." Crap. I wonder if we could follow Olivia to her house. We could get one of those long-lens cameras and try to get pictures of her at her computer, doing scandalous things with all the secrets. Like paparazzi.

"Samantha!" a voice cries. I turn around. Emma. Great.

"Oh, hey," I say. "What's up?" Ever since Emma con-fessed to me that she was going to the Fall Festival with Jake, and ever since I found out that she told Olivia about what happened with Barb, I've kind of added her to the list of people I'm avoiding. (And okay, yeah, the list isn't that long. In fact, she and Jake are the only two on it. But still.) I haven't answered her texts, I've made sure that I'm in class before she is, I don't go down the hallways where I know she's going to be. I've been forced to talk to her a little bit in homeroom, but that's about it.

"Samantha," Emma says, pouting out her bottom lip. "Are you avoiding me?"

"No," I say. "Um, not really."

"I called you, like, fifty million times!" She plops herself down on the bench between me and Daphne.

"My phone's been dead," I lie.

She looks at me skeptically. "Anyway," she says. "I am sooo tired. I've been like, nonstop running around trying to get ready for the Fall Festival tonight." She pushes her long curls out of her face forlornly, like she can't deal with the stress of trying to get ready for a seventh-grade school event. "By the way, Daphne, we're totally going to wear our cowgirl hats to school on Monday, so make sure you wear yours."

"I'm not going as a cowgirl," Daphne says.

"Yes, you are," Emma says. She reaches over and grabs the bag of chips Daphne's holding, then pulls one out and pops it into her mouth. "If the money's a problem, just tell me. I can give you back the twenty dollars." She rolls her eyes.

"No," Daphne says. "It's not the money. And I'm not going with you." Uh-oh. I thought Daphne had already told Emma about this.

"I don't like plans getting changed at the last minute," Emma says. "Besides, I already told my mom to pick you up." She leans back and pulls up the bottoms of her jeans, revealing caramel-colored cowboy boots. "Aren't they cute? I figured I'd wear them to school so I could break them in."

"Well, I'm sure your mom won't mind that she doesn't have to come and get me," Daphne says lightly. She reaches over and takes the bag of chips out of Emma's hand. Wow. Things are getting really tense around here. I look down at the ground.

"No," Emma says, her voice tight. "Probably not. But we need to have three cowgirls."

"You don't *have* to have three cowgirls," Daphne says.

"Yeah," I chime in. "It's not like the Three Musketeers or the Three Stooges or something." I meant it to come off as light, like *Oh, look, you don't have a costume that really requires three people*, but Emma turns around and glares at me.

"Two cowgirls isn't as fun," she says. She turns back to Daphne. "And if you don't dress as a cowgirl, you can't come with us."

"I don't want to go with you," Daphne says. "I'm going with Michelle."

"Michelle who?" Emma asks. She sounds totally bewildered, like she can't fathom the fact that not only is Daphne not going with her, but that she's going with someone named Michelle. I take a chip out of Daphne's bag and chew on it nervously. I don't think this conversation is going in a very good direction.

"Michelle Josephson," Daphne says. "We're going as soccer players."

"Michelle Josephson?" Emma snorts and pulls her jeans back down. "You're kidding, right? Daphne, come on, that's not exactly going to help your social status, now is it?"

Uh-oh. So not the right thing to say.

Daphne's hand tightens around the bag of chips she's holding, and a few of them crunch as they crush under her grip.

"Well, whatever," I say, forcing a laugh. "I'm sure you guys will run into each other at the Fall Festival and maybe you'll have some punch together or something." I stand up and try to grab Daphne's hand. "But we should get you off to the newspaper office; you're going to be late."

"Well, whatever," Emma says. She rolls her eyes. "It's fine, I don't care if you go with Michelle to the festival. I just didn't want Charlie to have to be left alone, since I'm going to be spending a lot of time with Jake." She tilts her head and thinks about it. "But I guess she'll be fine. Now that you're not going, more boys will probably talk to her."

"Yeah, so, we'll see you later," I say again. I'm standing

up completely now, and pretty much trying to yank Daphne off the bench. Seriously, I'm really yanking. I'm pulling the sleeve of her coat and everything.

"Bye," Emma says. "Just make sure you and Michelle don't have too much fun without me." She sounds like she's trying to make a joke. A really snarky, semi-mean joke that makes it sound like Daphne and Michelle are maybe the least fun, most lame people ever. And so Daphne turns back around. Crap. I was *this* close to getting her out of here.

"All right," Daphne says, her tone getting dark. "I've kept quiet about this for too long, but now . . . now this has gone just FAR ENOUGH." Her cheeks are red and she pushes the sleeves of her coat up. Wow. I've never seen Daphne like this. Are Daphne and Emma going to get into a fight? Am I going to have to break it up? God, I hope not. There's no way I'm strong enough to separate the two of them.

"Watch it, Daphne," Emma says, standing up from the bench. Her voice goes all steely and scary. "You don't want to say something you'll regret, now, do you?"

"Oh, trust me," Daphne says. "I won't regret it." And then, before I have time to even realize what's going on, she whirls on her heel and looks at me. "Emma knows you like Jake."

"What?" I shriek.

"Yup," Daphne says. She crosses her arms over her chest. "She knows. She's known since the sleepover. And she continued to pass notes to him anyway, she continued to *go after him* anyway."

"I didn't," Emma says, shaking her head. "I don't know what she's talking about, Samantha, I swear." Her blue eyes are wide and innocent.

"But she . . . How would she . . . ?" This is way too much information to be given all at once, and I'm trying to put it all together in my head. Emma knows I like Jake? And she's known this whole time? But how could she possibly? The only person who knows I like Jake besides me is Daphne. And *I* certainly didn't tell Emma, and I can't imagine Daphne would ever in a million . . . I turn to look at Daphne.

"I told her," she says quietly. Her lower lip trembles, and she looks down at the ground. "It was an accident, I didn't mean to, I just . . . It slipped out; I thought she already knew."

I look at Emma. "Is it true?" There's a huge lump in my throat, and it's making it hard to talk.

"No," she says, shaking her head vehemently back and forth. "Why would I have asked him to the Fall Festival if I knew that you liked him?"

"I don't know," I say slowly. "Maybe because you liked him too?" It all starts to click into place. The way Daphne was acting all weird after the sleepover. How Emma told Olivia what happened with Barb. It's true—Daphne told Emma I liked Jake, and Emma went after him anyway. So basically I have one friend (Emma) who I thought was my friend but never really was, and another friend (Daphne) who told my biggest secret.

"No," Emma insists, shaking her head some more. "I wouldn't do that."

"Why would I tell you that I told her unless it was true?" Daphne asks. "Why would I risk you being mad at me?"

"She's lying!" Emma yells. "And anyway, it doesn't matter. I mean, even if I did know you liked him, I didn't do anything wrong. He doesn't like you like that, Samantha; I asked him."

Warm tears spill down my cheeks, and I wipe them away angrily with the back of my hand. "I'm sorry," I say. "I . . . I have to go."

And then I push past both of them, ignoring them when they call my name. I walk out of the courtyard, down past the circle in front of the school, and onto the road. And then I start to run.

sixteen

I RUN ALL THE WAY HOME. IT'S TWO miles, and I am not a runner, not even close, and so by the time I get home, my legs are on fire, and the bottom of my jeans are completely soaked and muddy. The worst part? Now I have the super fun task of figuring out how to finagle this whole thing with my dad and Tom for the *You Girl* dinner tonight. I'm hoping I can spin it as some sort of weird, last-minute mix-up.

But when I get to my house, no one's home, and there's a note on the counter:

Dear Samantha,
Tom is working late, but will be home around six,
so that should give you plenty of time to still get to
the banquet on time. He will change into his suit at

work, and pull into the driveway and honk for you,
so please be watching and ready to run out to the
car. Good luck! I will be with you in spirit. Please
call me as soon as you find out and text me lots of
pics!! I am so, so, SO proud of you no matter what,
always.
I LOVE YOU,
Mom XXXO

Great. I guess I'll have to tell my dad first. He's going
to be heading to the banquet right after work, and he
thinks I'm getting a ride there from Tom. That part isn't
a lie; he just doesn't know that Tom is going to be staying there with us. But when I try his cell, I get his voicemail. Figures. I hang up without leaving a message. I
mean, what would I say? "Oh, hi, Dad, just so you know,
Tom's going to the *You Girl* banquet even though I know
you hate him and last time you talked to him you hung
up on him, see you tonight, kisses!"

I really wish Taylor were here so we could talk about
all of this, but she has cheerleading. I think about texting or calling her, but she won't get it until practice is
over, and by then Tom and I will probably be on our way
to the banquet. Ugh, ugh, ugh.

I trudge upstairs, where I spend the next hour getting

ready and trying not to think about what just happened with Emma and Daphne. I soak myself in a bath filled with bath bombs and glitter bubbles, then pull my hair back into a sleek ponytail. I have a simple black shift dress to wear, with black shoes that have a little bit of a heel. I wanted to wear a red dress, but my mom and I agreed this was more professional. Not that it really matters, since we picked my outfit over the weekend, way before the whole Barb-at-my-school debacle and before I realized there was no way I was going to win the *You Girl* award, red dress or not.

Once I'm ready, I go downstairs to wait for Tom. I eat a blackberry yogurt and then reapply my lip gloss. And right when I'm putting on my third coat of gloss and starting to feel really sorry for myself, I have an idea. A completely, totally, crazily brilliant idea!

Maybe there's a way for me to keep them apart! Neither my dad nor Tom knows that the other one is going to be there. So maybe I don't even have to tell them! That way, my dad won't know that I invited Tom first (or at all), and Tom won't feel like some kind of charity case I couldn't uninvite! Of course, it will take some finagling on my part, and Nikki will probably have to help me, but . . . it could definitely work. Feeling cheered, I dump the empty yogurt container in the garbage.

The sound of Tom's horn honking comes through the window, and I take a deep breath, then run out of the house and into the car.

The lobby of the King Tower Hotel is absolutely insane. Seriously. Complete and total chaos. I've never *seen* so many people—the *You Girl* staff, all the finalists and their parents, some photographers from the magazine (no sign of Tony, though; I guess this banquet is too important for freelance), and a bunch of girls who are too young to qualify for this year's contest but won their way in as spectators. Everyone is all dressed up. My mom would be happy to know that it seems like a lot of the finalists brought their moms, since she thinks that business is a male-dominated industry. I take a couple pics of girls standing with their moms and text them to her, trying not to feel sad that she's not here.

"Well!" Tom says, looking around and taking it all in. He's practically beaming. I feel a little sorry for him, actually. It's like he thinks I'm some kind of celebrity or something. "There's the check-in desk," he says. "We should get you all checked in."

"Good idea,' I say. I'm looking wildly around the lobby for my dad. Luckily, he is late to pretty much every single thing I've ever invited him to, so hopefully I'll be able to sneak Tom in, get him settled in at a table, then somehow get back out and grab my dad. And then, you know, get *him* settled in somewhere. Preferably somewhere far, far, away from Tom.

"Yes, hi, I'm Samantha Carmichael," I tell the woman who's in charge of checking everyone in.

"Let's see," she says, peering over her large glasses. She takes our tickets and then starts going through this box of file folders, one with each finalist's name on it. "Carmichael . . . ," she's muttering, moving at about the speed of a snail. Obviously she doesn't know my dad could get here at any moment.

I spot my folder, then reach over and pluck it out of the box.

"Got it!" I say. "Thanks so much!"

The woman looks a little stunned, but honestly not as stunned as she would be if my dad showed up and there was some kind of huge scene. My folder says I'm at table six, so I hustle Tom through the doors of the banquet room and over to our table. In a wonderful stroke of luck, table six is buried in the back corner. On the table is a little card that has "Samantha Carmichael" written on it in silver calligraphy. Next to it, there's a matching card with my dad's name. "Richard Carmichael," it says. Oops. I pluck it off the table and drop it onto the floor.

"That was a little rude, Samantha," Tom says as he sits down. "To grab your file folder like that right out from under that woman's nose."

"Uh, sorry," I say. "I was just anxious that we were going to be late!"

"You were?" Tom asks uncertainly. He looks around the empty banquet room. A few people are scattered around, talking and sitting, but for the most part, we're pretty much the first people in here.

"Anyway!" I say. "I gotta go to the bathroom! You stay here so that I don't lose you." I give him a pat on the shoulder.

"Okay," Tom says, still sounding uncertain. Hopefully he's writing my insane behavior off as nervousness. I mean, people do crazy things when they're nervous. Like all those people on *American Idol* who forget the words to their songs, or the way Olympians can totally choke at the last minute. Grabbing a file folder out from under some lady's nose is nothing when you really think about it.

I head back into the lobby and find the bathroom, where I've made plans to meet up with Nikki. She's already there, looking gorgeous in a navy blue dress. Her long dark hair is held back on the sides with two jeweled clips, and the rest falls to her shoulders in loose curls.

"Hey, Samantha!" she says when she sees me, enveloping me in a hug. She smells really good, like some kind of fruity perfume.

"You look gorgeous," I tell her.

"Thanks," she says. "So do you." She rummages around in her sapphire clutch and pulls out her extra ticket. "Here you go," she says, handing it to me.

"Thanks," I say. I look down at the ticket, my mind racing.

"What's wrong?"

"Nothing," I say, "It's just . . ."

"Oh, no," she says. "You didn't tell them they were both going to be here!" She gives me an exasperated look, but not in a mean way. It's more of a Samantha-what-am-I-going-to-do-with-you? kind of look.

"Not exactly," I say. Nikki knows all about all the drama between Tom and my dad. I told her in our emails. Although how she knows I didn't tell them they were both going to be here is beyond me. She must be pretty intuitive. I guess you have to be, to be successful in business. And from what I can tell, unlike mine, Nikki's business is booming.

"Well," she says, sounding determined. "You'll just have to make sure that you sit them on completely opposite sides of the room." If she's fazed by the fact that I've invited two guests and not told them about each other, she doesn't show it.

"Right," I say, thinking about it, "but the problem is, there are place cards."

"Place cards!" She says it like it's the craziest thing she's ever heard.

"I know, right?" Seriously. It would be such a shame if place cards were the death of me. It just doesn't seem right.

"Well, we're going to have to get rid of them," Nikki says.

"Well, I already ditched my dad's," I say as we head out, hoping no one steps on it and then ventures down to see what it is. I've had enough of people stepping on papers they're not supposed to see and ruining my life, thank you very much. "And the good thing is, I'm sitting all the way in the back." And at that moment I spot my dad, standing over in the corner of the lobby. He's wearing a black pin-striped suit and standing with his back to me, looking out through the huge floor-to-ceiling windows at the front of the hotel. Probably looking for me. Crap, crap, crap.

"That's my dad," I say. "And my stepdad is already in there."

Nikki bites her lip. "Didn't you say your stepdad is cool?"

"Ye-es," I say slowly.

"Well, maybe you could tell him that your dad just showed up here or something. You know, like you didn't invite him but he just came. You and your dad can sit wherever I'm supposed to be sitting, and I can sit with Tom."

"Ohmigod!" I say. What a brilliant idea! I can tell Tom that my dad just showed up, like some kind of weird crazy person, and that it's totally embarrassing, and now I need to keep him happy by sitting with him. That way, Tom won't have to know that I actually invited my dad, and my dad won't have to know that Tom is here at all!

"You're brilliant," I tell Nikki, grabbing her in a hug and spinning her around.

"Hey, hey," she says. "Careful of the dress." She smooths down her hair and smiles. "And besides, you can't call me brilliant until tomorrow."

"Why tomorrow?" I ask.

"Because that's when I'm going to be sending you a mock-up of your new website," she says. I squeal.

Then Nikki and I sneak back into the conference room to break the news to Tom. (The file folder lady totally gives us a suspicious look as we go by, which, in my opinion, is kind of not necessary. I mean, you grab one folder and she, like, holds a grudge.)

"Hey," I say to Tom.

"Oh, hi." Tom's drinking something out of a fluted glass. It looks like sparkling water. Leave it to Tom to order a water when we're in a super fancy banquet room with free drinks.

"Tom, this is my friend Nikki."

"Hello, Nikki," Tom says.

"Hey, Tom." She hops into my chair.

"Tom," I say, looking at him seriously. "We have a bit of a . . . situation here," I say, lowering my voice, hoping I can convey the seriousness of it. "Um, my dad's here."

Tom looks around. "*Richard's* here?" he asks wildly. His eyes sweep across the room, like he's afraid my dad might be stomping through the door, about to start threatening him or something.

"He's in the lobby," I say. Then I shrug. "He just showed up here; I didn't even know!" I almost add on "honest," but decide that would be going too far.

"Well, you're going to have to tell him to leave," Tom says. He nods his head and takes a sip of his water.

"Yeah," I say. "I could do that. Or . . . or I could just, um, sit over there with him, in Nikki's seat."

Tom looks across the room to Nikki's table, which is filling up fast. Then he looks at Nikki, who gives him a grin. And then he looks at me. "At Nikki's table?" he asks.

"Yeah," I say. "I mean, that way there wouldn't have to be a big scene. We could still spend time together, don't worry, I could change seats back and forth." Of course, I can't really do that (how would I explain it to my dad?), but I'm hoping Tom won't call my bluff.

Tom hesitates. "Samantha, I hate that you have to be put in the middle like this." He chews his lip, and for a second, I'm afraid he might insist on calling my mom. "So I suppose it's okay." He sighs. "And why don't you just sit with your dad for the whole night?"

"Are you sure?" I ask, trying to seem like I'm at least a little bit sad. Which I actually am, since I would much rather be sitting with Tom. Especially when they announce the winner and that winner isn't me.

"Samantha, the important thing is that I'm here to see this moment with you, and I don't have to be right next to you to do that."

He squeezes my hand and I head out into the lobby to get my dad, pushing down any feelings of guilt I have left.

My dad is annoyed because he had to wait in the lobby for so long. Even though *he's* the one who's always late, he's annoyed with *me*, who was on time. The first one in the banquet room, even! Of course, he doesn't know that.

"Sorry, Dad," I say, breathlessly. "I just got here."

"Why couldn't Tom get you here *on time*?" my dad asks as we make our way through the throng of people into the banquet room. "What was he *doing*? Probably spending all his time putzing around, with no regard for anyone else's schedule."

How about working late and then getting settled in at table six? But I don't say anything. We take a seat at our (Nikki's) table after I do a quick , covert sweep of the place cards. I order a virgin pina coloda (yum) from our waiter, and soon after, the lights dim and the program starts.

"Hello," Barb says from the podium. "And welcome to the sixteenth annual *You Girl* Young Entrepreneur of the Year banquet."

Everyone claps. Then Barb goes through a whole slide show, announcing each of the finalists and our businesses. When she shows mine, I'm glad to see there's a picture of me standing in front of my locker, I'm not blinking, and nothing is mentioned about my fake secrets. They serve us a dinner of roast chicken and these adorable little baked potatoes, but honestly, I'm way too excited to eat. Although I do sample a cookie from the dessert tray. (They're these delicious frosted cookies in the shape of a magazine, with our names and the year in chocolate icing. I'm never too nervous to eat chocolate.)

Then Candace gets up to give a speech, which I will summarize here:

"Me me me, I'm so awesome, Darfur, me me me, here's how to order some bracelets."

Then our special guest, a woman named Daisy Halverson, gets up to talk. Apparently she's this super important real estate woman who's made like millions and millions of dollars even though she started her business with, like, close to nothing. She talks about how important it is to instill a sense of entrepreneurism in the girls of today. Honestly, the whole thing is a teeny tiny bit boring. I mean, I like business and everything, but I'm not sure I want to *dissect* it so much. My dad, however, is totally riveted, staring at the stage, nodding at everything that Daisy is saying, and clapping in all the right places.

Finally, it's time to announce the winner of the *You Girl* contest, and Barb reclaims her place center stage.

"All of our girls tonight are winners," she says into the microphone. "Just taking the initiative to conceive of an idea and take the necessary steps to put it out there makes you miles ahead of other girls your age." She gives the whole group a big smile.

My dad looks over at me then, and I see the excitement

and anticipation on his face. And then, just for a second, I let myself think that maybe I could win. Maybe I will win the *You Girl* contest, maybe Barb won't hold against me what happened that day, maybe she'll—

"And the winner," Barb says, "of this year's *You Girl* Young Entrepreneur of the Year award is . . . Nikki Geraldi!"

Everyone claps, and Nikki heads up to the stage to get her award, and I'm so happy for her that I leap out of my chair and I'm clapping and yelling her name, and I'm sad that her family isn't there to see her. So I take, like, five million pics of her on my cell phone so that she can show her mom later.

And when I sit back down, I look over at my dad. He looks surprised, probably because he can't figure out why I'm so happy that someone else won. "She's my friend," I explain.

"That's nice," he says. And he's clapping, and then he reaches over and squeezes my shoulder. But I can tell he's disappointed.

On the way out, that woman Daisy is standing in the lobby. She's shaking hands with some of the parents and talking to some of the girls, who are falling all over her like she's some kind of celeb or something. I see Candace getting a picture with her, and an autograph. Of *course* she would be. What a suck-up! Whatever. I'll bet she didn't even know who Daisy was until she got here.

"Come on," I say, pulling on my dad's hand. "We gotta get home, it's a school night!" I texted Tom after dinner and told him to let my dad and me leave first, that my dad would drive me home, and that Tom should wait until every single person is out of that banquet room before he comes out, so that I'm sure to be gone. I cannot believe I might actually get away with this. It wasn't even that hard.

"It's not a school night," my dad says. "It's Friday."

"Well, I have this new thing where I treat every night as a school night," I tell him. "That way I make sure I don't upset my sleep rhythms."

"I want to talk to Daisy," my dad says.

Oh, for the love of . . . I look over my shoulder nervously to see if I can catch a glimpse of Tom. But so far, he hasn't come out. Daisy's now sitting at the check-in table, and a line has formed in front of it. Seriously. A line. You'd think she was, like, a rock star or something.

I reluctantly join the line with my dad. It inches forward sllloowwly, and I go slowwwwly crazy. When it's finally, finally, finally our turn, my dad and Daisy start chatting away like old friends—something about the real estate market and how brave she was to get into it when she did, and how she must be really smart and savvy to withstand this economic downturn, and blah blah blah.

I get a picture taken with her, mostly because I think my dad wants me to, and then, finally, they're wrapping it up.

"Come on," I say, pulling on my dad's hand. "We gotta get going."

"It was so nice to meet you, Samantha," Daisy says. She reaches into her purse and pulls out a business card that she hands to my dad. "And, Richard," she says. "Feel free to call me if you ever have any business questions. We should have lunch and talk shop."

My dad tucks the card into his suit coat. "I will definitely do that," he says. "Sooner rather than later."

Oh my God. Gross! My dad is hitting on Daisy! No, actually, *Daisy* was hitting on my dad first, and now my dad is flirting back with Daisy. Eww! I'm completely over the whole "maybe my parents will get back together" thing, but it's just sooo disgusting when you see your parents flirting. It's, like, not natural or something.

"Nice to meet you, Daisy," I say again, pointedly. I resume pulling my dad toward the door. Now that he has Daisy's number, he can call her anytime he wants and doesn't need to keep chatting her up, so, miraculously, my dad follows me. The lobby is almost completely empty now, and we're almost at the door, we're two steps away, even, when I feel my dad's fingers get tense around mine.

"Come on," I insist, giving his arm another pull. But my dad stops.

I turn around. And there's Tom, coming out of the banquet room. My dad looks at Tom. Tom looks at my dad. My dad looks at me. Tom looks at me. I look at my dad.

"Dad—" I start. "I can explain, look, he just—"

But my dad drops my hand, turns around, and walks out of the lobby.

The problem is that when you sort of kind of stretch the truth to your dad, and then you sort of kind of stretch the truth to your stepdad, your mom is always able to find out how you stretched the truth to each one. She just gets the story from the two dads, and voilà.

Which is how I end up in my kitchen that night, sitting at the table with my mom. And she is *not* happy.

"Why would you do something like that?" my mom wants to know. "Lie to your father and Tom?"

"I don't know," I say, looking down at my hands. I feel so, so awful. Like, more than awful. "I just didn't want anyone to be mad at me."

"Well, unfortunately, that mission has not been accomplished." My mom throws her hands up into the air. "Because now *everyone* is mad at you, including me."

"I know," I say. I feel like I want to cry. How did this happen? I mean, I've pretty much alienated everyone that was close to me. Now that my friends are total traitors, and Jake likes Emma and not me, I have no one but my family. And now even *they're* mad at me. I wonder if I can transfer to Nikki's school. At least *she* still likes me. "It was just . . . I mean, I invited Tom, and I really, really wanted him to go with me. But then it turned out that Dad could go after all, and then I couldn't exactly tell him why he couldn't, so . . ."

"How did you even get two tickets?" my mom asks. She's up and pacing around the kitchen now, her ponytail flying behind her.

"I got one from my friend Nikki," I say. "Her mom couldn't go, even though she totally won." I beam at my mom, but she doesn't seem pleased.

"You're grounded," she says.

"Mom!" Then I realize it doesn't matter. I have nowhere to go anyway. "Fine," I say, sliding back in my chair.

She holds out her hand for my cell phone. "No cell," she says. "And no computer."

"Mom!"

"No," she says.

I have no choice. I hand over the cell and head up to my room.

Seventeen

TAYLOR IS THE ONLY ONE I HAVE LEFT.
The only one who loves me. The only one who knocks on my door the next morning to see if I'm okay. At least, that's what I *thought* she was doing. Turns out she just wants me to go with her to pick out a dress for the homecoming dance.

"I'm grounded," I say miserably. "So, sorry, I can't." Doesn't she know that I need to wallow in my own misery? I go to push my bedroom door shut on her, but she wedges her hand between the door and the frame. "It's okay," she says. "I got special permission from Mom. She doesn't want me going to the mall by myself, but if you go, I guess it's okay or something." She rolls her eyes, like the idea of me being her chaperone is the most ridiculous thing she's ever heard.

"Where are all your friends?" I ask.

"Oh, please," she says. "No one else is up this early."

"Then why are you?"

"Because," she says. "I don't have my dress yet, and if I don't go now, then I can't go later, because I have cheer-leading practice all weekend, and tomorrow is Sasha's birthday party." She rolls her eyes again like maybe I should already know all this.

"Fine," I say, figuring it's better than lying in bed and obsessing over what happened with Emma and Jake at the Fall Festival. And how I have no friends left. And how my whole family minus Taylor is mad at me.

I throw on jeans and a sweatshirt, then meet Taylor downstairs.

At the mall, she drags me from store to store, trying on dress after dress. Long dresses, short dresses, dresses in every single color and style. You'd think it would be boring (and slightly annoying—how many dresses can one person try on?), but honestly, after the first few, I start getting into it.

"You should try one on," Taylor says, after two hours of her flouncing in and out of dressing rooms. So far, I've strictly been a spectator, rating the dresses Taylor tries on in three categories—color, style, and home-coming appropriateness.

"But I'd have nowhere to wear it," I say.

"Doesn't matter." She shrugs. "Do you really think I can afford some of the dresses I tried on? Plus obviously some of them are so totally homecoming inappropriate. It's just for fun."

So we try on dresses and laugh and act silly and probably drive the salespeople completely and totally crazy. We make up these ridiculous fake names where Taylor calls me Isadora and I call her Cornelia and we pretend we're sisters who are visiting from England and we even talk in these fake British accents. And before I know it I'm giggling and laughing my way through each dress, and kind of forgetting about what happened with Emma and Jake, with Daphne, and with my dad and Tom.

Until we stop for milkshakes at Shake It.

"I'm going to have the pumpkin shake, Cornelia," I say, then crook my little finger in what I hope is a very British way. "It's the only thing that will do at this time of the year." I slide the menu back in between the napkin rack and the wall.

"That sounds quite delicious, Isadora," she says. She turns to the waitress. "Oh, excuse me, darling, we'd like two pumpkin milkshakes tip-top!"

"Tip-top?" the waitress asks, giving her a disbelieving look.

"Yes, darling, that means right away," I say. "You Americans are so funny with your language!"

"Yeah, whatever," the waitress says, rolling her eyes and going to get the shakes.

I burst into giggles, and so does Taylor, but when we stop laughing, she looks at me seriously.

"You have to talk to Dad," she says.

My stomach does a flip. "What do you mean, Cornelia darrrling," I try. "You mean our father, the Duke of Ellenbury?"

"I'm serious," she says.

I reach over and fiddle with the menu. "There's nothing to say," I tell her. And why is she bringing this up now? I don't want to talk about anything to do with my dad. I want to be Isadora from England, darn it.

"Yes," she says. "There is. You need to tell him about what's been going on with your business." I open my mouth to protest, but she holds up her hand and keeps talking. "I mean what's *really* been going on, not just an overview. And you need to let him know that you're only doing the secret-passing thing for fun. And that yes, you like the business side of things, but that you're only in seventh grade, and you need to have some fun, too."

"I can't say all that," I say. "Dad will be crushed!"

"And most of all," she goes on. "You and I both need

to talk to him about the way he is with Tom."

"I don't know," I say. Neither one of those conversations sounds like one I want to have. The waitress reappears and sets down our shakes.

"Two pumpkin milkshakes," she says. "Tip-top."

"Thanks," Taylor says in her real voice. The waitress shoots her a weird look before disappearing back behind the counter. "Dad and Tom don't have to be BFFs," Taylor says. "But we have to do *something* so that we don't feel so totally uncomfortable about the situation. I mean, we've never told Dad that it bothers us. At least I haven't, have you?"

"No," I say, squirming around on my chair. The thought of talking to my dad about how I feel is pretty upsetting. Of course, a lot of bad things have been happening because of the fact that I didn't want to tell people how I felt. If I'd just told Emma from the beginning that I liked Jake, then maybe I would have known all along that she was a backstabber. If I'd told Jake I liked him, maybe things wouldn't be so weird between us now. And if I'd told my dad about what was going on with my secret-passing, maybe last night wouldn't have been such a disaster.

"Look, talking to him can't be any worse than what's already going on, can it?" Taylor asks.

"I don't know," I say. I take a big sip of my shake out of the special jumbo straws they give you at Shake It.

"We can do it together," she says, then reaches over and takes my hand.

"Okay," I say, giving it a squeeze. "I'll try."

The waitress comes back over and puts the check down in front of us.

"Thank you, darrrling," Taylor trills. "Now I will have to figure out how many pounds this check is; that is what they use in England, you know."

"My grandmother's from England," the waitress says. She looks annoyed. "And that, darrrling, is the worst fake accent I've ever heard." She turns and walks away, and Taylor and I burst into giggles. And we don't stop laughing for a long time.

On Monday, I avoid Daphne in the hallways. Emma ignores me in homeroom, laughing and talking with Charlie. Jake looks over at me a couple of times, but I don't look back. I just pretend I'm working on homework. I still have no secrets in my locker, and in kind of a last-ditch effort, I spend all day trailing Olivia, but again, I don't catch her doing anything.

I do the same thing on Tuesday, but the whole thing is pretty futile. And besides, even if I *did* catch her reading a secret, what would I really do about it? I still don't have my cell, so it's not like I could snap a picture of her or anything. It would be her word against mine, and honestly, who's going to believe me? Everyone knows her business is beating mine.

By the time Wednesday rolls around, I've given up on following Olivia. I decide that the thing I need to focus on is making *my* business better, not trying to discredit hers, even though what she's doing *is* pretty despicable. I just have to trust that people will eventually start figuring it out on their own, the way Eric and Karissa have.

The good news is I'm able to check my school email account from the library (I'm still grounded from the computer at home, but my mom has no control over the school computers, now, does she?) and Nikki's sent me a mock-up of my website. It's absolutely gorgeous! All aquas and shades of blue and purple, with big swirly letters that spell out SHHHHH! all across the top. I am ecstatic. I can't wait for it go live in a few weeks, and I can't wait to show—well, I guess Taylor, since no one else is really speaking to me.

Every chance I get, I'm back at the computers in the library, staring at the mock-up. Which is where I am on Wednesday morning when I feel a pull on the back of the hood of the pink zip-up I'm wearing.

Daphne.

"Hi," she says, sliding into the chair next to me.

"Bye," I say, starting to gather up all my things and put them in my bag. Daphne's made a couple of attempts to talk to me over the past few days, but honestly, I'm over it. I don't want to talk to her. Not now, not ever. Every time I think about her telling Emma I like Jake, and then keeping it from me for so long . . .

"No, wait," Daphne says. "I need to explain."

"Nothing to explain," I say, taking my bag and sliding it over my shoulder. "You told Emma a secret that was not supposed to be told to anyone, under any circumstances, *ever*."

"I know," she says, biting her lip. "But, Samantha, I swear, it just sort of slipped out. I would *never* tell one of your secrets on purpose, and *especially* not to Emma."

I start walking quickly toward the exit, but Daphne follows me. "Wait," she says, stepping in front of me and blocking my path. "What would you do if I told you that I have proof that Olivia is reading secrets?"

I scrutinize her face for any sign that she's lying in an effort to get me to talk to her, but there's none. "Tell," I say. "And do it quickly."

"First you have to listen to what happened with Emma," she says.

"No."

"Then no proof." She stares at me. I stare at her. It's like a stalemate, with each of us waiting to see who's going to blink first. I think about it. On one hand, even though I said it wasn't really about bringing Olivia down anymore, it *would* be nice to have some proof that she was doing shady things. On the other hand, I don't want to have to listen to Daphne, because I'm still really mad at her. On the *other* other hand, I do kind of miss her. Daphne, I mean.

"Fine," I say finally, narrowing my eyes at her. "But make it quick."

Daphne leads me over to a table in the back of the library.

"Like I said," I say, still not completely ready for this. "Make it quick."

"Okay, so the night of the sleepover," she says. "While you were getting your makeup done with Charlie." She looks down at her hands. "It just . . . slipped out. Emma kind of tricked me into thinking she already knew."

"And how did she do that?"

"She said, 'So what's the deal with Samantha and Jake; how long has she been in love with him?' and so I thought you'd told her. And so I said, 'Well, they've been best friends forever, but they just started liking each other.'"

"You made it sound like Jake liked me, too?" I ask, pleased in spite of myself.

"Of course," she said. "I didn't want her to think that she could just swoop in and steal him!"

"So then what?"

"So then she goes, 'I doubt that. I mean, it was obvious from the way Samantha looked at me when I passed Jake that note that she likes him, but I really don't think he's interested in her at all.' And then I knew. That she didn't know." She's still looking down at the floor, and her green eyes look all watery, like maybe she might start crying.

"Why didn't you just tell me you told her?" I ask.

Daphne doesn't say anything, and so I start to stand up.

"No!" Daphne says, grabbing my sleeve. "Wait! Look, I wanted to tell you, but I couldn't. I felt like I was getting squeezed out everywhere. You and Emma and Charlie were becoming friends, and I thought you and Jake were going to be a couple. I was losing everyone! She wasn't a good friend, Samantha, but I couldn't tell you because I didn't want you to find out I told her. And I didn't want you to think I was just being jealous." Daphne's eyes are filling with tears now, and I feel my heart melt a little bit. This whole thing must have been really hard on her.

"I would never have done anything to hurt you. I

thought Emma would eventually tell you that she knew you liked Jake, or that you would tell her on your own." Daphne wipes away her tears with her sleeve. "I'm so sorry, Samantha."

I feel myself melting even more. I mean, honestly, who am I to judge someone when they make a mistake? I've gotten myself into a lot of my own messes lately. Plus I can tell Daphne really is sorry. She hardly ever cries. "I really, really wish you would have told me sooner," I say.

"I know," she says. "But I was scared of losing my best friend completely."

We're both crying now, and I reach over and hug her. "It's okay, Daphne," I say, "I forgive you."

"I missed you so much," Daphne says. "I've been calling your cell, like, nonstop."

"No cell," I tell her. "I'm grounded."

"You are?" she asks. "For what?"

I fill her in on what happened at the *You Girl* banquet. Every single, solitary, sorry detail. "Geez," she says.

"I know." I look down at my hands for a second, then decide to ask her the question I've kind of been dying to know. "So how was the Fall Festival?"

"I didn't go," she says. "Michelle's grandmother got

sick, so she had to cancel. And obviously I wasn't going to go with Emma and Charlie."

"That sucks," I say. "I'm really sorry you didn't get to go."

"It's okay." She looks at me, her eyes shining. "So do you want to see what I found out about Olivia?"

eighteen

DAPHNE TAKES ME TO THE NEWSPAPER office, which is really just an old English classroom with a bunch of computers and a copier. There are a couple of other kids there, including Eric Niles.

"Samantha!" he says when he sees me. "How are you? Do you need a drink? I could run to The Common and get you a lemonade. Or maybe you're hungry. Here, do you want some of my muffin?" He holds up something that looks like a gray rock with icing on it.

"Uh, no, thanks, Eric," I tell him. "I'm fine."

"Okay." He looks disappointed as he goes back to working on his computer.

"Now," Daphne says. "I'm glad we got to be friends again before I show you this, because once you see it, you are going to love me forever."

She pulls a picture out of a manila folder, and sets it down on the table.

"Are you showing her? Are you showing her?" Eric says, bouncing over to the table we're at.

"Yes, Eric," Daphne says, rolling her eyes. "I'm showing her."

"But you said you weren't going to show her until you two were friends again." Eric takes a bite of his muffin, and crumbs get all over his green button-down shirt.

"We're friends again," Daphne says.

We all crouch over the picture. It's black and white, one of those random shots that gets taken for and put in the school newspaper or the yearbook. It shows Marissa Murphy and two of her friends with their arms around each other, smiling into the camera. And over her shoulder, in the background, is Olivia. She's leaning against her locker, reading something on a halfway folded-up sheet of loose-leaf.

"You can't see it," I say. "You can't see what she's reading!"

"No," Eric says, grinning from ear to ear. "You *couldn't* see it." He rushes over to a computer in the corner and pulls something up on the screen. "Until I blew the picture up."

I bend over and peer at the screen. In this shot, you

can clearly see that Olivia's reading something that says, "Dear Marcus, want to go to the Fall Festival? We can do more than pumpkin pick, if you know what I mean, wink, wink, XXXXXO, Love, Karissa."

"It's Karissa's secret!" Eric yells, stating the obvious.

"Yes, I see that," I say. My heart is leaping with joy. "Daphne," I say, "you're a genius."

"It wasn't me," she says. "Eric's the one who found it and blew it up."

"I took the picture too," he says, blushing.

"Eric!" I say. "I thought you didn't know that much about computers. How did you know how to blow this up?"

"Well," he says, "after that day in The Common with Jake, I figured it might be time to learn a thing or two."

"You guys," I say, "are awesome."

Daphne beams.

Eric beams.

And I get ready to figure out what I'm going to say to Olivia.

"Tell her you're taking her down," Daphne instructs a few minutes later. The first bell is about to ring, and I'm waiting at Olivia's locker, getting ready for her to come out of The Common. I know she was there before school because we sent Eric by the caf to do a little recon mission. "Tell her you're not going to put up with her anymore, and that if she ever starts with you again, you'll—"

"Daphne!" I say, holding my hand up. "I'm not going to do anything violent!"

"Of course not!" Daphne says. "I just meant that— ooh, here she comes." Daphne looks down the hall over my shoulder. "I'll be right over there. And don't let her intimidate you."

"I won't," I say. My stomach is flipping over and over again, even worse than it does when Jake is close to me.

Olivia walks up to her locker and starts to spin the dial, and I lean over and tap her on the shoulder. She turns.

"Oh, hi, Samantha," she says. She places her white fluffy coat into her locker, and then checks herself in her locker mirror. "Are you coming to ask for a job? Because, honestly, people have kind of started to talk about how you lost the *You Girl* award, and I'm not sure your name is so good in the secret-passing business anymore." She smiles sweetly. "You're kind of, like . . . *disgraced.*"

"I want you to shut down your business," I say.

She laughs. "Why would I do that?" she asks. "Everything's going so well." She looks over my shoulder, dismissing me. "Hey, Emma!" she says. "Let's walk to homeroom together."

Emma comes bounding over. Ugh. I should have known those two were friends now.

"Hey, Samantha," Emma says. Her voice sounds fake-nice. "How are you doing?"

"Fine," I say tightly.

"That's good." She gives me a smile that matches her tone—fake, fake, fake. "I've been wanting to call you, but I thought I'd leave you alone until you got over your anger." She waits for me to say something, but I don't. "So, ah, are you over it?"

"No," I say. "I'm not over it. In fact, it's getting worse."

"But, Samantha—"

"Look," I say, turning my back on Emma. I look at Olivia. I had this whole big speech planned where I was going to get her to break down and admit what she did, but honestly, I'm a little thrown off. I thought she would be a little snarky, yeah, but I had no idea she'd be so down-right mean. Not to mention that now that Emma's here, I really need to speed this up. I don't want to be around her, since who knows how long it's going to take before she brings up Jake. And I really do not want to hear about *that*.

So finally I just pull out the picture Eric took and wave it in front of Olivia's face. She looks at it, and her smirk dies. "Where did you get this?" she demands. She grabs it out of my hand and then rips it in half. "Where did you get this?" she asks again.

"Don't worry about it," I say. "And it doesn't matter that you ripped it, I have tons of copies." I'm not completely sure about that, but since the picture is saved on the newspaper computers, I'm pretty sure I'm right.

"Let me see that," Emma says. She picks up the two halves of the picture, puts them together, and gasps.

"What do you want?" Olivia asks me. Her voice sounds shaky, and her face is bright red.

"I want you," I say, "to shut down."

"Shut *down*?" Emma gasps. "But we were just getting started!" I turn around and look at her. And then I get it. Emma's friends with Olivia now because *Olivia* is the one who has the successful secret-passing business. In fact, that's probably the only reason she wanted to be friends with me in the first place. And when I wouldn't read the secrets, she latched on to someone who would.

"Fine," Olivia says quietly. She looks down at her shoes. "And you won't show this to anyone?"

"I won't show it to anyone," I say. After she shuts down her business, what reason will there be? I turn and start to walk toward my homeroom.

"Wait, Samantha," Emma calls from behind me. "Can we talk?"

"No," I say. I keep walking.

At the end of the day, I'm at my locker getting my stuff ready to go home. And that's when I see it. One secret. In the front of my locker. My heart does a little leap, and I get excited. There's no way that word could have gotten out about Olivia already, is there? I reach into my locker and pull out the folded-up note with the dollar on it.

As my hand wraps around the paper, I realize how much I miss having secrets to pass. It's fun, especially when the person you're passing to gets a really good one. I look at the name on the front. "Samantha Carmichael," it says. I look around, thinking it might be a trick from Emma or Olivia. But they're nowhere to be found, and so I unfold the paper. All it says inside is "Meet me on the soccer field after school."

I fold the note up and slide it into my bag.

"Hey," Daphne says, coming up to me. "So I'll meet you at four o'clock?"

Daphne's going to her newspaper meeting, and I had planned to do my usual thing of hanging out at The Common and waiting for her so that we can catch up on all the news we missed from not talking for the past four days. Since I'm still grounded, hanging out at The Common is a perfect way for me and Daphne to be able to hang out.

"Look at this," I say, showing her the note. "Do you think it's from Emma or Olivia?"

She reads it. "Probably from Eric," she says, rolling her eyes. "He probably has some sort of big romantic candlelight picnic planned or something to celebrate what happened this morning. You should go and humor him; he was really nice to blow up that pic for you."

"It's not his handwriting," I say.

"He probably got someone else to write it for him." Daphne shrugs. "You know how much he likes surprising you."

"True," I say, sighing. The last thing I want to do right now is have a picnic with Eric. But at this point, honestly, I need all the friends I can get, and Eric helped me sooo much this morning with that picture.

So when Daphne heads to newspaper, I head out to the soccer field. It rained last night, and so the field is a little muddy, and my shoes make squishing sounds as I walk across the grass. But when I get to the soccer field, no one's there. I decide I'll give Eric five minutes, and then I'm leaving. Hopefully if it *is* a picnic he didn't make the food himself, and just got it from Whole Foods or something. I have a feeling a homemade Eric picnic might not be all that edible.

I pop a Jolly Rancher into my mouth, pull my social studies book out of my bag, and start to read. A minute later, I hear the squeak of someone's shoes on the grass. I look up. And almost choke on my Jolly Rancher.

It's Jake.

"Hey," he says. He stands in front of me, his hands in his pockets, his shoulders slightly hunched, a sheepish look on his face.

I close my book. "Hi," I say.

He pulls something out from behind his back. One flower. One pink carnation with a long stem.

"This is for you," he says. I take the flower. I've never gotten a flower from a boy before. In fact, I've never gotten *anything* from a boy before. Jake sits down next to me on the bench, our legs touching.

I swallow. "What about Emma?" I ask. "I mean, aren't you guys—"

"No," he says. "I'm not with Emma. I never was." He takes a deep breath. "Didn't you get all my texts and messages?"

"I don't have my phone," I say. "I'm grounded."

"For what?"

"Long story."

"What about emails?" he asks. "I emailed your personal account."

"Haven't checked it," I say. "Only my school email, since I got my computer time taken away too." He nods and we don't say anything for a second. Then he reaches out and takes my hand. Oh my God, oh my God, oh my God. Jake. Is. Holding. My. Hand.

"Listen, I never liked Emma," he says. "Not in that way. I always liked *you*. Over the summer, when I was at camp? I couldn't stop thinking about you. I don't know, it was like . . . something had changed between us."

Yes! I knew it! Something did change between us that day! I knew he felt it too. But still. That doesn't change the fact that we almost kissed and then he blew me off. Or the fact that he was passing secrets with Emma. "But, you and Emma were passing all those secrets," I say. "And you decided to go to the Fall Festival with her." I'm looking down at the ground, halfway afraid to look at him. It's not that I don't believe what he's saying . . . it's just that it doesn't make sense. Plus, it's enough of a distraction that he's holding my hand. No way I'm going to be able to keep my wits about me if I look at him.

"The secrets were mostly about you," he says. "About whether or not she thought maybe you liked me."

"Why didn't you just ask Daphne if I liked you?" I

finally look at him, and he looks at me, and it's just like that day with TSSI, only better.

"Because I knew Daphne would tell you," he says. "And I didn't know if you liked me back." He blushes. "And the only reason I told Emma we could hang out at the Fall Festival was because she told me there was a chance you were going to meet up with her later."

"But why didn't you just tell me that when I asked you about it that day we got into our fight?" He's sitting really close to me now, and I can smell the cologne he's wearing, and I can feel the softness of his fleece jacket against my arm.

"I was embarrassed," he says. "I didn't know if I wanted you to know how much I really liked you. Emma said in her notes that you *didn't* like me, and then she asked me if I liked you, and I said yes. I figured she would tell you at some point, and then I'd be able to figure out how you really felt. It was all so confusing, especially after that day in my room when we were looking at Olivia's website. I just . . . I don't know, I freaked out." He pulls his hat off and swings it around, so that the brim is facing backward. I remember that one note I read, the one that simply said "yes," and my heart does a flip. Jake wasn't saying yes about liking Emma. He was saying yes about liking *me*.

Jake grins. "Any more questions?"

"Two more," I say. "One, why are you finally telling me this now?"

"Because when you wouldn't talk to me, I realized how much I really missed you."

"Good answer," I say.

Jake's grin gets bigger. "What's the second question?"

"So I didn't imagine it when . . ." I take a deep breath, "When, um, we almost kissed? You really did want to?"

"Yes," he says. "I really did want to." And then he's moving closer toward me, and his lips are right there, and they look soft and kissable and I don't have time to think before he brushes them against mine. And this time, it's definitely not my imagination.

Daphne and I spend an hour and a half in The Common talking about what just happened outside on the soccer field. ("Did you like it?" "Was he a good kisser?" "Are you guys, like, boyfriend/girlfriend now?" "Does this mean I'm a third wheel?" Yes, yes, yes, and no.)

We get so caught up in our conversation that we totally lose track of time and Daphne's poor mom is waiting outside for, like, twenty minutes before we get in her car and start heading home. When we pull onto my street ten minutes later, I'm still smiling.

"Any chance your mom might give you your cell back tonight?" Daphne asks hopefully.

"I think so," I say. "My grounding's supposed to be over tomorrow, so she might give me a pass."

"Cool," Daphne says. "I'll call you so we can discuss." She gives me a meaningful look, one of those *You know what I'm talking about but I can't say it in front of my mom* kind of looks.

"Okay," I say, throwing her a grin.

"We have a lot of *things* to talk about." She raises her eyebrows up and down and we both collapse into giggles.

"What is going on with you two?" Daphne's mom asks, shaking her head. "Seriously, you guys have had the giggles the whole way home."

"Nothing, we're just, you know, *giggly*," Daphne says. Which makes no sense but for some reason makes us giggle even more.

Daphne's mom pulls up to my house, and suddenly, my smile disappears and my heart drops. Because my dad's car is in the driveway, and he's sitting on our front porch. Taylor and Tom are with him. Oh. My. God.

"Uh-oh," Daph says, turning around in the front seat and looking at me. "You gonna be okay?"

"Yeah," I say, even though I don't know if it's true. "I'll be fine."

I thank Daphne's mom for the ride and then jump out of the car, my heart beating all crazy in my chest.

"Hey, Dad," I say as I walk up the driveway.

"Hi, Samantha," he says. He's wearing his suit, and he stands up and slides his hands into his pockets.

"Dad picked me up from cheerleading and, uh, I thought maybe we could all talk," Taylor says. "If that's okay with you?" She looks nervous, like I might go crazy on her for springing this on me with no notice. And honestly, normally I probably would. But I'm in too good of a mood. And besides, ignoring the problems with me and my dad and with my dad and Tom isn't going to make them go away.

"Come on," I say, giving them all a smile. "Come inside and I'll make everyone a snack."

I don't know why, but all of a sudden I just know that everything's going to be okay. I'm going to work things out with my dad. I'm going to figure out how to make my dad and Tom at least be able to be in the same room with each other. And if nothing else, I'm going to tell them how I feel. And then I'm going to bring Taylor upstairs and tell her about my very first kiss ever.

I push open the door and my family follows me inside.

"Now, who wants a Nutella sandwich?" I ask.

"Me!" Taylor says.

"Me!" Tom says.

My dad hesitates, then says, "Me."

I pull down the jar of Nutella, the loaf of bread, and four paper plates. And then I sit down at the table and get ready to tell some secrets.